DEATH

FROM DOWN UNDER

JAMES E. AARONS DVM

A KATIE REYNOLDS ADVENTURE

Books by James Aarons
Fear of Failure
(My Autobiography)

Katie Reynolds Adventures
Butterfly Boy
Yéiitsoh Omen
Death from Down Under
Tsegi Ruins
The First Altar

Inconvenient Goddess
Of Gods and Mortals
Queen of the Orontes
The Ivory Kingdom

Yezidi Holocaust
The Tiger Lady
Cocaine Eggs
The Sandman
The Devil Hunters
Goddess of Death

Acknowledgements

I wish to thank my tireless editors, Brian Ortiz and Jon Wolfson, for the hours of painstaking review and suggestions they have given me.

Thank you, Stephanie Laird, for your beautiful photography.

And I wish to fervently thank Mary, my wife, for pushing me into new frontiers by allowing softer and gentler things to be shown in a book dominated by a male psyche.

Thanks, mate! Accolades for my Aussie friend, Janice Konstantinidis. Your invaluable authentication gives me confidence the book will be accepted Down Under.

Thank you

2/
7/2019

Table of contents

Chapter 1: Suddenly Alone
Chapter 2: Splenectomy
Chapter 3: Pounder
Chapter 4: San Francisco
Chapter 5: Mile High Club
Chapter 6: Sydney To Gatton
Chapter 7: Billy O'Rourke's Station
Chapter 8: Jen's Bathtub Soak
Chapter 9: Australian Bats
Chapter 10: Billy's Roast
Chapter 11: Paint Wars
Chapter 12: Carrie Comes to Visit
Chapter 13: Visit Brisbane
Chapter 14: Jocko
Chapter 15: Gatton to Sydney
Chapter 16: Release from Quarantine
Chapter 17: Sugar Gliders
Chapter 18: San Francisco
Chapter 19: Honey and King
Chapter 20: Sugar Glider Babies
Chapter 21: Hoof Abscess
Chapter 22: King's Fever
Chapter 23: Dr. Troy
Chapter 24: Necropsy
Chapter 25: The Carnage Continues
Chapter 26: The Diagnosis
Chapter 27: Katie Arrives
Chapter 28: Jen is Home Alone
Chapter 29: Final Goodbye
Chapter 30: Carrie Arrives
Chapter 31: Montana de Oro
Chapter 32: Back to Australia
Chapter 33: Another Colic

About the Author
The Katie Reynolds Series

Chapter 1

Suddenly Alone

Walking through the empty stalls, Jen was overwhelmed by the horror of the past few days. Now the place felt haunted. She needed to be with others.

She waved to the deputy guarding the quarantine area, watched him pull down the Do Not Cross yellow tape and drove out of her ranch. Parking in front of Twin Cities Hospital, she went through the front door and walked to the isolation area. Rory was already there, holding Susan, Troy's wife, who sobbed in Rory's arms.

"What happened?"

"Troy passed away from pneumonia early this morning," Rory said.

Jen started shaking. "What about my husband? What about Victoria?"

"She's okay so far. IV therapy will give her the edge she needs to fight this thing," replied a nurse near the group.

"Why did Dr. Troy die in spite of your excellent IV therapy, then?" Jen asked, irritated.

"It all depends on how many infectious particles a person is exposed to. Evidently, Dr. Osborne was too close to the situation for too long. His body could not kick out the infection even with support."

Jen was unnerved as well as angry. There would be no guarantee Randy or Victoria would be coming home either.

"Can I see my husband?" Jen asked the nurse.

"Yes, I will show you how to wear a PPE suit. You'll also need to wear a mask, and if you want to touch the patient, you must have gloves taped to the sleeves of the gown."

Jen's mood darkened as the nurse assisted her in putting on the protection suit. *I need to get past this. I need to be there for Randy,* she thought. Jen put her chin up, smiled, and walked into the isolation room. She ignored all of the equipment, the monitors, and the tubes that were attached to Randy "Hi, baby. I miss you," she said through her forced smile.

He nodded in recognition.

Randy was fatigued and not always coherent. Jen didn't want to burden him with the reality of the situation. She sat with him a long while. At times he dozed off and woke up complaining of head and muscle aches. Periodically, a nurse would come in to check Randy's lines and monitors. Jen closed her eyes and focused inward reliving the last few months to better understand the tragedy. It all started when she took Pounder to Australia.

Chapter 2

Splenectomy

Doc Rory Evans and his assistant Honey sat on the office countertops enjoying coffee between procedures. Rory, a young, sturdily built man a few inches shy of six feet tall with sand-colored hair, wore a mustache he thought made him look older and more distinguished. His manner was sometimes gruff, but always entirely honest. Some people didn't like him because he made them uncomfortable with his artless ways. However, others trusted his skills and abilities. He was a good vet and had a way with animals. He understood them and could quickly figure out what was ailing them. His patients couldn't talk, and he sometimes wished their owners couldn't either. It was a rare occasion to see him outside without his white, Resistol hat perched confidently on his head.

Honey, twenty-one years old and 5 ft 8 inches tall, had curly blonde hair. Her sea-green colored eyes and her freckled face were the first things you noticed about her. She had been working as Rory's office manager and assistant for just over two years. Rory was entering his third year as a licensed veterinarian. Having spent his first year at a clinic across town, he realized he needed his own clinic if he were to stay in the area because his personality clashed with the fellow who hired him fresh out of vet school.

His desire to have his own practice solidified when he met Jen, a young woman his age who grew up in the area. Her uncle had been a vet in the small town of Paso Robles for years, but the clinic was forced to close when the fellow was killed in a car accident on his way to an emergency on a foggy winter's night. Hoping her acquaintance with Rory would grow into a romance, Jen facilitated the renovation, but she couldn't move the young doctor's focus away from Katie, his vet school sweetheart. After a contrived dalliance with Rory in the shower, Jen realized he was still in love with his far-away girlfriend.

Knowing how hard Jen worked to set him up with an office, Rory remained friendly and warm, but was careful not to find himself in another awkward situation with her. He hoped having his own office would calm Katie's worries about settling in California. Katie was a Navajo, a Native American who had gone to vet school intent on returning to the reservation. But those thoughts faded somewhat when she fell in love with Rory.

Feeling pressured to settle, Jen rekindled her part-time relationship with Randy, marrying him after her try with Rory failed. Jen thought it was a good move in spite of Randy's age. The marriage helped quench the forever-alone fear many young people have. Plus, Randy's maturity and strong sense of family gave her the freedom to continue exciting animal endeavors, like riding the Tevis Endurance ride, and raising Chesapeake Bay Retrievers.

"Doc, Jen wants me to move to the ranch as soon as possible," Honey said.

"I thought you liked living upstairs," he replied. Rory worked out of a modified barn with the vet clinic downstairs and a one-room apartment above where Honey lived. "It's rent-free. Why do you want to move?"

Honey and Jen were related. They were cousins and shared the building as a family trust.

"You know all those dog shows, Jen's been going to?"

Rory nodded. "For her Chesapeakes?"

"Yeah. Well, Jen's got this opportunity to make a lot of money with it, but I need to watch her place for a month."

"I'm afraid to ask," Rory chuckled, shaking his head. "Okay, tell me."

"She's going to Australia. She'll tell you as soon as she's inside, that's her truck pulling in."

Suddenly the door burst open. A big, happy, brown dog dragged Jen into the reception room, vigorously wagging his tail. The dog looked like a chocolate-colored Labrador but with a shiny, tightly whorled coat.

"This is Pounder, Rory. He's the dog I'm shipping to Australia." Jen was an attractive, petite woman in her late twenties. Her body was toned from years of riding horses. Her light brown hair was cut in a short bob, and her eyes were a disarming light grey with glints of yellow that flashed when she teased, which was often.

"So, this is the newest up and coming breed?" Rory nodded thoughtfully. "Hmmm…"

"Hmmm what Rory? Do you have a problem with Chessies?"

"Yes, er… no, I like him, Jen. When did you become so sensitive?"

"Not sensitive, just anxious to get this breed off the ground. It was a spur of the moment decision, but now I've become a big Chesapeake Bay Retriever breeder. And this fellow here is my connection to the Australian funding for my next project."

"Along with five hundred other things, I'm sure."

"Those other things are on hold. I have seven Chessies now, and they take up most of my time. I call this fellow Pounder. Jocko, his father, is an AKC champion. I finally earned enough points for him to become nationally known."

"Why Chesapeakes, Jen? I've never seen any others here; not many people know of them."

"They're becoming better known now on the west coast. I've made lots of friends. Plus, it put me on the world radar. That's how I snagged Mr. Australia. The tough guy Aussie mindset has discovered the Chessies, and I'm not surprised. Chessies are perfect with their can-do attitudes and kick back aloofness. They are calm dogs that pique the minds of the type of people that interest me."

"Why doesn't the fellow buy a puppy from one of the breeders in Australia?"

"He wants the best. I convinced him only the U.S. has the best Chessies."

"Really? I thought this was a breed from England. It should be well known in Australia."

"Nope, one hundred percent American, Rory. The Chesapeake Bay retriever came into prominence in the 1850's in West Virginia to help bird hunters retrieve their day's catch. They crossed Newfoundlands with water spaniels, setters, and hounds. I like them; they aren't as goofy as Labs or Goldens, they're more interesting."

"You're telling me a breed is interesting? You're so invested in this idea you sound like a peddler."

"Oops, sorry. My salesman side is slipping out. I've been spending too much time developing contacts, and it's time for a break. That's why I'm here."

Squatting to pet Pounder, Rory grabbed the happy brown head, steering it up and down using the ears as handholds. "Hi there, Pounder." He laughed at the goofy face. "Oh, you're a really special guy."

Pounder responded well to verbal praise, wagging his tail vigorously. His sparkling relaxed eyes showed approval at Rory's attention.

"We're just about to go into surgery," Rory said. "Should we put Pounder in a kennel or can he just hang out? Have you trained him to be good in the house?"

"He's trained, he'll lie quietly." Jen looked lovingly at her puppy. "I'll get his blanket from the truck. That will tell him where his place is."

"Have you taught him Australian?"

"I don't know Australian other than 'Hiya mate' and 'G'day.' Do you?"

"Not really," he smiled.

"I'll be right back with the blanket."

"And change into scrubs so you can gown up with me," Rory yelled. Jen sometimes helped Rory with busy days and hard surgeries.

"Okay, Honey, bring Zoey over, Rory said. "It's time to catheterize her."

He helped Honey lift a sizeable black lab onto the table, and she took the position across from him.

"Ready?" He asked.

Honey nodded and snaked her left arm around Zoe's head and pulled it into her chest. With her right hand, she leaned across Zoe's back to grab the dog's right elbow.

"Hold the vein off, grab the elbow tightly," Rory instructed.

Rory took Zoe's right paw, turned the clippers on, and shaved the top of Zoe's leg allowing him to clearly see the cephalic vein which was now bulging from Honey's handhold at the dog's elbow.

Rory smoothly inserted the two-inch catheter into the distended vessel until blood flowed from the open end. Plugging it with a catheter cap, he flushed the blood back into the bloodstream by injecting saline through the cap.

"One final check," he said listening to the heart with his stethoscope. "Okay let's drop her." The sedative worked faster when given IV. In less than a minute Zoe's eyes became unfocused, and her head fell to the table.

Lifting Zoe's head, Rory opened her mouth and peeked inside. "Let's use a 10.5 endotracheal tube, Honey."

She handed him string along with the clear breathing tube he requested and took over the head grab, freeing up Rory's hands. Picking up the laryngoscope he turned on the light at the end of it. Now he could see into the back of Zoe's cavernous mouth.

"Keep her nose high," he said. With Zoe's mouth hanging open Rory pushed the ET tube to the back of the dog's mouth paying extra attention to thread it through the vocal cords. The vee-shaped vocal cords told him he was in the trachea, the airway to the lungs, and not the esophagus, the route to the stomach. Next, he used the string to tie the tubing to Zoe's upper jaw. That way the tube wouldn't accidentally slide out.

"Okay let's flip her over, it's time to shave the belly."

"Whatcha need Rory?" Jen came from the bathroom wearing scrubs.

"Help Honey get Zoe on the surgery table to prep her. I'll start washing in. We have to gown up for this procedure," he said, showing Honey how big of a patch he wanted her to shave on Zoe's belly. Walking to the surgical prep sink, he scrubbed his hands with sudsy soap using a brush to get them nice and clean. He went through the same routine on each side starting at the fingernails and finishing at the wrists.

He opened the sterilized gown pack and picked up a sterile towel to dry his hands. With dry hands, he grasped the folded gown at the neck lifting it in front of him as he stepped backward. Honey had wrapped it correctly; he could easily find the armholes. After working his arms into the sleeves, he worked gloves onto his hands from the inside, using the cuff of the gown to keep his bare hands covered while his fingers pulled the gloves on.

Between the gloves and the full-length, long-sleeved surgical gown he was able to completely cover his front in a sterilized manner from his neck down to his knees.

"Can you tie me?" He asked Jen, who was setting up for a similar wash procedure.

Jen tied his neck first then cinched his waist and placed a bowtie at the small of his back.

"There you go," she said.

It was not quite right for Rory's taste. "Can you pull the hem down Jen?" He asked.

"Pardon me?"

"The hem, I hate wrinkles in my gown; it distracts me."

"You're kidding me, Rory! You should try wearing dresses with slips and nylons for an entire day," she said laughing as she pulled his hem down to his liking.

"No thanks, I'll see you in surgery." He walked out keeping his hands folded together in a praying pose. It was the cleanest way to move through the room.

"How's Zoe doing Honey?" Rory asked when he walked through the surgery door. He heard the steady beep, beep, beep of the respiratory monitor, a welcoming sound. When breathing stopped for more than a minute, an alarm went off. The dog was lying on her back, her four feet tied to the surgery table to keep her long body from tipping side to side. The shaved patch on her belly was colored brown from the betadine spritzer Honey added as the final prep.

"She's good. Her breathing is stable," Honey replied.

Rory nodded. "Open the surgery pack and table drape pack, then go tie Jen up. I'll get started," Rory said as he took his place on Zoe's right side.

Rory placed four sterile towels to outline the surgery site on top of the belly, securing them to each other and the skin using

15

sharp pincher clamps. The towels were secured onto the patient when the pincers were closed. The towels maintained a sterile barrier around the surgery site that wouldn't move.

Returning to the drape pack, Rory picked up the final curtain, a big folded piece of material. He waited for Jen to assume her place across the surgery table.

"Ready to place the drape?" He asked.

"Sure," Jen nodded and extended her gloved hands to his. Sharing the material, they opened a large four by six-foot drape with a rectangular hole in the center, called a fenestration, through which the surgery is performed. Everything around them was clean, sterile actually, not even a single, contaminating bacteria in sight. Rory breathed a relaxed sigh. Besides maintaining sterility another effect of the drape is a visual one. Now the only thing in front of Rory was the surgical area placing him in a highly charged and very focused world. Right now, in this place that's all there was for him.

"All set?" He asked.

Jen nodded, as Rory set a cutting blade onto his scalpel handle. She armed herself with white gauze sponges and they went to work. He had done this many times. There is a midline on a dog's underside. The less he strayed from the midline, the easier the surgery went. That's why table positioning was critical. Zoe was on her back inside a V-shaped cradle. She was steady and straight, perfect positioning for a splenectomy.

Jen dabbed bleeders with gauze while Rory cut into the skin. He used Metzenbaum scissors to cut away some of the fatty, underlying connective tissue. Metzenbaum are perfect tissue scissors; they have blunt tips, so they don't poke into things, and the blade is curved allowing for a smooth bite into slippery, moving, living tissue. He completed his arsenal with a pair of rat-toothed forceps. The teeth on these forceps, two on top one on the bottom, allow secure tissue pickup. Now Rory had the tools necessary to pick and cut his way through different tissues. And he had an assistant and an anesthesiologist/floor nurse to keep the patient asleep and hand him stuff when he needed it.

The cut through the skin exposed underlying subcutaneous tissue, the white stuff that keeps our skin connected to our body.

Rory scissored away the subcutaneous junk, mostly fat. Now with the skin cut open and the fatty tissue cleared away he could see the best place to enter into the animal's abdominal cavity.

"There's the white line Rory," Jen said pointing to the line running down the middle of the stomach from the xiphoid to the pubis.

"Yep, the linea," he replied. He set the scissors down and picked up his scalpel blade. Using his rat-tooth forceps, he lifted the tissue.

"Why do you tent the linea?" She asked.

"I need to push the blade through the body wall with enough force to open a space for the scissors, but I don't want to nick the bladder or spleen, or something else. I would need to repair it before I sew out. It's sloppy and unnecessary."

Satisfied with his knife opening, he grabbed the scissors, pushing one end inside Zoe's belly.

"Now watch how I slide the Metzenbaums along the white line, opening the belly with more of a push than a scissoring. That's how sharp the scissors are."

Jen didn't have much sponging to do. There were few bleeders cut, as Rory did not stray from the white line. Finding the tumor was easy because it was so large. The hard part was to open the incision enough to pull the grapefruit-size thing from Zoe's belly. The mass was so big Rory had diagnosed the thing yesterday just by feeling the dog's stomach.

His tugging on the tumor sent painful wake-up waves to the dog and Rory backed off.

"Turn her isoflurane up, Honey. She's too light." By dialing the gas level higher, Zoe went into a deeper anesthetic plane within ten breaths. Dropping both hands all the way inside the belly Rory began to ascertain the attachments the tumor had with other abdominal organs.

"Yep, this confirms it, it's on the spleen. We're going to have to remove the spleen too. That means we need more carmalts and more clamps. There are ten to twenty large blood vessels we need to ligate. First, we need to get the spleen, and the tumor exteriorized. You ready to manhandle this thing, Jen?"

She nodded. Her hands were ready, waiting on top of the drape. Rory worked his fingers deeper to cradle the mass. He lifted it gently and carefully lest he rip apart something important. Slowly working it back and forth he wrestled it from its nesting place.

"Wow it's immense," Jen exclaimed, as Roy pulled the softball-size mass through the incision.

"Put your hands down here and cradle the thing, Jen. I have to work the spleen out too. Then we need to lay it out and ligate the vessels going to it."

"So, the tumor isn't attached to anything else besides the spleen?"

"Correct, Jen. There's some omentum adhered to the cancer ball, but that rips away with no bleeding, see? Yep, the tumor is only attached to the spleen. In fact, part of it is growing from the spleen itself. We need to tie off lots of vessels, remove the sucker, then sew her back up."

"Why do you need all the clamps?"

"It saves me half the work. When I ligate a vessel, I have to place two ties an inch apart. Then when I cut the artery between the two ties, there will be no bleeding. If there are twenty vessels, I need forty knots. But if I have twenty clamps, I only need to ligate the portion I leave inside Zoe not the half going into the spleen. When the tumor is removed and thrown away, hopefully, Honey will remember to retrieve the clamps."

"Okay, I'm convinced. I like the clamp idea."

"Hand me another reel of 2-0 Vicryl please Jen."

"Did you look up the Australian import requirements, Doc?"

"You are serious, aren't you? Why do you want to go there?"

"Why do men want to go to the moon, Rory? This deal combines my love of dogs with my love of travel."

"It's the travel thing, Jen. Your big travel life has been a few months or so in Flagstaff, and then you come right back here."

"What makes you think that? Why do you think I never spend time in Flagstaff?"

"You let Katie and I stay there when I brought her back from the Rez remember?"

"So?" She sounded irritated.

"The place looks spanking new. It's not lived in at all. It's like a hotel room."

"Well, I'm feeling the travel urge now." She was tired of talking.

Rory sensed it and focused on the surgery again. "You need to move the spleen over. I have to ligate this section. Oh good, only three more. Hand me some 2-0 Monocryl on a needle and get ready for closure."

With the ligation finished they slid the mass into a container.

"Weigh this thing, please, Honey," Rory asked.

"It's twelve pounds!" she said setting it on the scale.

"Wow, that's a lot for a sixty-pound dog. It's like a forty-pound tumor in a two-hundred-pound man."

The rest of the surgery was uneventful. All that remained was to close up the surgery site.

"So, I'm ready to follow my travel urges." Jen was willing to talk about it again.

"But what does Randy say? Is he going too?"

"He's interested but not enough. I think he'd be a drag, and I'm not pushing him to do anything with me."

"I see," Rory said. "Hold the suture when I hand it to you. I need to make sure there is enough tension to close this running stitch. If not, I'll have to over-sew. Here, let's go back and tighten these earlier few."

"There's this element of salesmanship that's exciting for me Rory," Jen said. "Like riding the Tevis Cup you know? Raising these dogs that someone across the world wants to buy is like getting a buckle for finishing the Tevis. You never asked why I did that."

"Okay, okay, I'll stop asking."

"The dog contacts led me to this Aussie fellow," she smiled. "And I clinched the sale by suggesting the dude didn't know what he was doing with this particular breed. That will get them every time, hit them in their manhood."

"Oh, you have become vicious. Here grab the scissors so you can cut after each suture." Rory switched to simple interrupted sutures for the skin, which meant each one stood alone, tied and cut. The incision was long; he would need at least twenty-six skin sutures.

"Naw. Not really. I'm standing up for this beautiful breed, that's the way I see it. A lot of my concerns are true. These dogs need discipline, and I suggested that Aussie men might not have that discipline. I told him the dog has to be active every day swimming, running around, that type of stuff. Chessies need something to do, and the rough coat they have gets dirty easily, so the coat needs to be brushed often. I wanted to make sure he could do all that, and it set him off a bit."

"I'm surprised he didn't hang up on you."

"No, he took it as a challenge. He wasn't going to be stopped by a woman's opinion. That stuff never happens in Australia. But I persevered, telling him Pounder will strive to become the dominant alpha in his group. That's the way Chessies are."

"That's why you like them."

"You would too. You're high energy as well, Rory. So, I told Mr. Billy O'Rourke from Queensland he was going to have to become the dominant person as well if Pounder was to be fulfilled."

"Fulfilled! Did you say that stuff to him? Jen, he's not as arrogant as you think if you can talk to him about fulfillment and happiness in a hunting dog. That's not anything like the hunters I know."

"It's my charm, my political grace," Jen replied smugly.

"And he said okay, after all that?"

"Yep. Billy told me he wants the best. He's willing to pay for it too. I softened though when he said the dog was to be a birthday present for his son Mick."

"Oh okay, that makes sense."

She nodded. "In a few months when Mick turns twenty Billy wants to give him a dog to retrieve the birds they shoot. There are a lot of lakes there. Oh, and Billy says the Queensland Heelers they have are good cattle dogs but don't retrieve very well."

"I've never heard of any inadequacies with Queensland Heelers."

"Me neither. Billy's looking around for more toys; I think their lives are set. Billy's family has had the ranch since the 1850s. It's a large, working cattle ranch outside of Gatton in Queensland. His great, great, great grandfather Patrick came from Ireland to grow potatoes. Eventually, the potatoes were replaced with fields of alfalfa, he calls it lucerne.

I had doubts about sending Pounder so far away and rewrote the contract half a dozen times. I finally came to a workable solution. I offered to bring the dog to Australia myself. Billy agreed to pay for the flight and the month-long quarantine because that's the kind of guy he is. I'm feeling good about it."

Chapter 3

Pounder

"Let's focus on Pounder Jen," Rory said after they finished Zoe's procedure. "We have a lot of paperwork and lab work ahead of us if you're serious about this trip."

"Of course, I'm serious! With the amount of money Mr. O'Rourke is willing to pay me, I see it as a paid vacation," she smiled. "I want to do this thing, Rory."

"First you'll need a veterinary certificate stating the dog is physically fit for such a long trip. I need to sign the form within ten days of the flight."

"Okay."

"The rest of the requirements are dictated by the Australian Quarantine and Inspection Service the AQIS."

"Why do we have to put Pounder in quarantine for thirty days?"

"Australia doesn't have some of the diseases we have here, and they don't want someone to introduce one."

"Like what?"

"Rabies, there is no rabies virus living in Australia yet, and the Australian government wants to keep it that way."

"Well, why can't we test for it and let him go if he's clear?"

"Some diseases may be in the very beginning stage of their infection, and blood tests might miss these infected animals. By putting them in quarantine for four weeks, the people in the station will retest for the disease before they let him go."

"I see…"

"Good, first Pounder needs a microchip put under the skin at the back of the neck."

"He already has that. You put one in when you gave him his second set of vaccinations remember?"

Rory flipped back through the record and saw Jen was right.

"And he needs to be vaccinated against rabies within the last twelve months. We gave him his rabies shot three months ago, so that's fine. I'll have Honey make you a copy of the rabies certificate as well as his microchip number."

"Okay."

"And a rabies blood test needs to be done."

"Why does he need a blood test even though he's vaccinated?"

"To make sure the rabies vaccine has worked to induce adequate protection. The test looks at the antibodies against rabies. We need to make sure Pounder is producing enough of these, so we will draw blood today."

"Splendid."

"Blood must also be drawn to make sure the dog is not carrying various other diseases: ehrlichiosis, brucellosis, leishmaniasis, and leptospirosis."

"What are the chances he has any of those?"

"Almost nil but none of those conditions are in Australia, and AQIS doesn't want some dog from outside the country accidentally bringing any of those in no matter how small the possibility. It's their form of infectious disease insurance for their entire country."

"Anything else Doc?" Jen asked.

"Pounder needs to be current on regular vaccinations including distemper, parvo, influenza, and kennel cough." Rory flipped through the records. "Yes, he is current. I'll have copies made of these for you as well."

"Thank you."

"Within four days of export, he needs to be wormed for roundworms, hookworms, whipworms, and tapeworms. We've already done that, and the worming is repeated every month with him on heartworm prevention. Have you continued his monthly dosing?"

"Yes."

"Good, finally he needs to be treated for external parasites: fleas and ticks. You can use one of the flea and tick medications we give him every month to satisfy this requirement."

"Well, all that sounds doable Doc. I'm beginning to look forward to this trip."

"Not so fast. You have some homework. Before shipping, an appointment with the quarantine station needs to be made to ensure there will be space to accommodate Pounder during the quarantine period of thirty days. In Australia, the quarantine stations are in Perth, Melbourne, and Sydney."

"I want to use the Sydney station because Sydney is the closest of the three to Brisbane," Jen decided.

"Well, you need to call them as soon as you can."

Jen snapped to attention, smartly throwing Rory a salute. "Yes sir, Rory, sir."

Chapter 4

San Francisco

It was early afternoon when Jen's sister-in-law Janie drove her and Pounder to San Francisco International terminal.

"Jen, I have no idea why you're running off again," Janie told her.

"Don't get me started, Janie. Randy isn't ready for me; he's still obsessing over his last wife Donna, and she's dead."

"Maybe he feels guilty."

"He should; Donna died because of his stupid idea. They shouldn't have been out there hiking the Grand Canyon in stormy weather."

"So, you're off to Australia alone because you're mad at Randy?"

"Yes, and I'm surprised you don't want to come with me."

"David will only complain. It bugs him that you don't spend more time with Randy He thinks you should be more like me."

"What, stay home and wait on them?"

"Yeah, I guess. They don't want anything to be one bit different. Remember, last month, their mother wanted company on a boat trip to Cuba. It was her treat and neither David nor Randy wanted to go with her."

"Well, she could have asked one of her daughters-in-law. At least she likes you," Jen replied.

"Not really. You're gone a lot, so you don't know but I'm not close to Margaret either. You're my best friend on that ranch."

"And that tells you something right there. The two ladies that married into the family are still outsiders. There never was room for anyone else, Janie. They never accepted us."

"I don't think it's on purpose, do you?"

"No, maybe it's a lack of mutual interests. I always felt it was too out of Margaret and Pete's way to find out about me. They haven't even asked me of my earlier life. But I never made any effort to talk to them either, so I'm partly at fault."

"Well, I need you to know how special you are to me, Jen, and how much I'm going to miss you."

"I'll be back."

"Probably, but one day you won't. You'll find what you're looking for."

"What do you think I'm looking for?"

"I don't know, and I don't believe that you know either. That's why you run all over the place, and that's why you write books. You create other worlds; you want to be elsewhere."

"You would rather be somewhere else as well. That's why you start drinking the minute you get up."

"But I don't have the self-confidence you do Jen. You're the only person I know who decides what you want then goes out and gets it."

"But you just told me I don't know what I want."

"You don't right now, but you're not afraid to go looking. I am."

"Oh, here's the airport exit. Look for a parking lot near Qantas Airways," Jen said.

Before leaving for the airport, Jen placed Pounder in an altered crate with a water container fixed inside. The box would stay locked until arrival at the Australian quarantine site. She arranged proper bedding and watering devices to accommodate these requirements. The bedding was super-absorbent and the water dish filled from the outside.

"Wait here while I see where we need to go," Jen said. She grabbed her luggage but left the dog with Janie and went into the terminal.

24

"Hello," she said to the ticket agent. "Here's my ticket to Sydney and I'm bringing a dog in a crate as well."

"Very good," the woman replied. "You need to take the dog to the AQIS station. Follow the arrows to this building to process the animal, Ma'am. Use this flat cart to move the kennel," she walked further behind her counter to retrieve a wheeled flatbed buggy.

Janie helped Jen push the cart deeper into the catacombs of the airport. The AQIS office was close to the customs area. As Jen approached the counter, a young man appeared with an AQIS badge.

"How can I help you?" he asked.

"I'm taking this dog to Australia. Here's the paperwork. I believe I have done everything you need to get Pounder ready for import," Jen said.

The agent scanned the papers and stamped 'Approved.' He placed a 'Live Animal' sticker on Pounder's cage and sealed the door shut with a zip tie device. The sealed crate would be collected from the Sydney airport by AQIS staff and transported directly to the animal quarantine station.

To lessen any damaging influence on Pounder, Jen purchased a ticket for a non-stop flight from San Francisco to Sydney. Between the fourteen-hour flight time and the fact Australia lies halfway around the world Jen would board the plane at midnight Saturday and land in Sydney at 9:00 am Monday morning.

After Pounder was taken away for loading on the plane, Janie walked Jen as far as she was allowed to go without a ticket. They hugged, and Jen headed for the long snaking line of people waiting to go through the security stations.

"Excuse me Miss, is this your bag?" An English-accented voice asked. Janie turned to see two fellows, one wearing a curious brown hat. The thing was made of brown felt and had what appeared to be corks dangling from the brim. Janie quickly averted her glance afraid her reaction to the God-awful thing would be rude.

The tall one who spoke was pointing to Jen's carry-on.

"Yes, no not mine, it's Jen's. She stepped into line over there. She's the one wearing a cowboy hat."

"That way?" The second Aussie mate squinted and pointed.

"Yeah."

"Good that's where we're going too, c'mon Richard!"

The two ran after Jen. Janie smiled knowing Jen was going to have an enjoyable flight.

Chapter 5

Mile High Club

"Sheila! You've forgotten your bag!"

Jen smiled. Hearing the Australian accent immediately lightened her mood. She looked around for someone named Sheila, but she was the only female nearby. She saw two tall, handsome, tanned men looking at her with big smiles on their faces.

"Excuse me!" the cutest one said. "Is this your bag?"

"Oh, it is thanks. Where did I leave it?"

"At that last counter."

Her tired eyes became very shiny as she focused on the young men. "Thank you. My name is Jen," she said and held out her hand.

Both men stood tall, relaxed, and self-assured.

"G'day I'm Brolga," the cute one replied in a heart melting Australian accent. "I'm here with me mate Richard. We're from Australia."

"I can tell by your accent." Things were looking better by the minute.

Brolga was three to four inches taller than she. He had a sharp shock of strawberry blonde hair and freckles sprinkled all over his face. Richard looked to be five-foot-nine. They wore heavy hiking boots and warm flannel shirts with Levi jeans.

"How is yer going? I'm Richard," stated the other fellow with the hat still perched on his head. That made Jen giggle; Richard had wine bottle corks dangling freely, happily, and haphazardly from the brim of his hat. The entire effect was comical. Every time he moved his head the corks would hesitate a moment before being yanked along with the movement of the cap.

26

"What are those corks for?" she asked afraid to call them dingle balls lest she offend the fellow.

"This here's a cork hat. These corks here keep the flies and bugs away," he replied matter-of-factly. He removed his hat as he straightened up to shake hands with Jen. He had black hair and was thinner than Brolga.

"Where are you headed, Jen?"

"Sydney for a month then Gatton. It's up north somewhere."

"We're going that way too; we should stay together. What seat are you in?"

"First class 3A. And you?"

"Cheap we're in the tourist section 81 B and C I think…. Hmmm, let's see, yep."

"But we can still mingle, it's a long flight," Jen volunteered. She stayed to talk with them when the call came for first class passengers.

Brolga noticed. "Jen they're calling first class, go get your seat we'll mingle after take-off as you say."

"What do you like to drink? I'll order you one. They always ask me what I drink before I sit down, Brolga. What do you like?"

"Richard and I are taking a fancy to your California wines."

"What type?"

"You mean red or white?"

She nodded.

"White, fruity white wine, Gewurztraminer."

"I can do that. Take your time boarding. I'll get you a glass." She squeezed his hand before turning to queue up for First Class boarding.

Sure enough, she appeared in coach with two glasses of wine during the mild chaos of seating passengers.

"Thanks, Jen," Brolga said.

"You're welcome. I'll see you later when things calm down."

Jen dug into her bag to retrieve one of the sleeping pills Janie gave her. It would get her sleeping in ten minutes and keep her down for a few hours. She ordered a double gin and tonic and popped her pill.

Jen woke sometime in the middle of the night. The plane must have lurched her awake because the loudspeaker remained quiet. She looked outside. It was dark, nothing below but moonlit ocean. Beautiful, but very dull after the first few minutes. The flight attendants were resting, and most of the passengers were asleep.

She walked past the business class where guys in their suits were sleeping or working on their laptops.

In Second-Class she passed a couple playing cribbage. She walked to the back of the plane and there in seat 53C she came upon Brolga in a deep sleep. Richard was one seat over, and he too was asleep.

Smiling, she gently pushed on Brolga's shoulder.

"Oh! Hi there," he yawned sleepily. "What's up Jen?"

"I need you to see something Brolga. Come here, follow me." She took his hand, helping him to his feet. He took a moment to rub his neck and get the sleep from his head.

"What do you need Jen?"

She chuckled. "I need you, Brolga."

He smiled, nodded, and followed. There were bathrooms directly behind the boys' seats. She opened the door to the first but was dismayed at the cramped space, so she closed it, hoping the next restroom was bigger. It was. She smiled, turned, and pulled him in, sliding the lock to 'Occupied.'

Sitting her butt on the small sink, she turned and invited him closer pulling his face towards hers. She let their lips touch; then their tongues twirled together as she pulled him closer. She could feel his cock harden as he leaned against her leg.

She was wearing a blouse and skirt. Smiling, he unbuttoned her blouse, admiring her breasts in the lacy black bra. Popping first the right one then the left one free of the lace he kissed each nipple sucking briefly. She responded by grinding her hips into his crotch.

Her hand went behind his head, pulling him to her. "I want you in me," she whispered.

He pulled her skirt up and saw she had no underwear. Moving away from her, he kicked his shoes off and wiggled free of his pants. She laughed at his sexy shimmy as he worked his underwear off without bending down.

"Someone had us in mind when they designed the height of the sink," she murmured as she grabbed his hard penis, rubbing her clit and pussy lips with it.

28

Leaning back, she wrapped her hands around his bum and pulled him fully inside her. She wound her legs snugly around him and let him work his magic in the confines of the little lavatory. Orgasming simultaneously, the roar of the engines drowned out their moans. They kissed and dressed. He left the restroom first, closing the door behind him. As another person waiting opened it Jen stepped out causing the woman to do a double take. A stewardess looked at them knowingly and gave her a sly smile.

"Let's go up to the lounge," she said. "We can sit together there."

He followed her up a stairway to the sitting area with a snack bar. Jen poured herself a coffee and Brolga popped a beer open.

"The hats, you guys wear, seem flimsy Brolga," Jen said.

"Not so Sheila! They are much more useful than your cowboy hats, which need particular attention to keep them looking proper. These hats are called Barmah Oilskin Canvas Hats. They have chinstraps, so a gust of wind won't send them flying down the plains as your cowboy hats do. They are also crushable. Here watch this." Brolga pulled his hat from his back pocket put it on his head then took it off folded it and returned it to his pocket. "If an American cowboy hat got crushed this way the poor bloke would need to buy a new one next chance he got."

"Okay, so what are the corks for?"

"To keep the flies away. You should know that Sheila. You look like a cowgirl with your boots and hat. I'm surprised your hats don't have such conveniences."

"We're more into the image; our cowboys wear Resistol or ten-gallon hats, not floppy hats with used corks hanging from them. Why were you in the States, Brolga?"

"Richard and I went to see the cutting horse finals in Reno."

"You run cattle? I thought Australia was known for its sheep. I didn't realize you were beef eaters like us."

"Richard and I are Jackaroos or were. Now we are boundary riders, but we keep up with our riding and roping. And you're right about sheep. They are a big industry, but so is cattle-farming especially in the north, in Queensland. There are a handful of massive cattle stations up there. Sheep are more to the southeast. Now that Mad Cow Disease is in the United States,

Canada, and Great Britain, Australia is supplying beef to Japan, China, and South Korea."

"What is a boundary rider?"

"Richard and I are one of fourteen doggers. The Wild Dog Destruction Board pays us twenty-six thou a year for maintaining six-hundred kilometers of the fence, five days a week, all to keep the dingoes in Queensland and South Australia out of the grazing lands of the states west.

"Do you ride horses along the fence?"

"No. They started with camels, but there are roads now, so I take my Ute."

"What is a Ute?"

"The Ute's been Oz's favorite truck since the 1930's," he said proudly. "Ford Motor Company designed an Australian utility vehicle, forty years before SUVs were popular in the States."

"Why did you quit jack-a-rooing? Is that how you say it?"

"Money. The lifestyle's the same, being out in the middle of nowhere. But this position comes with a three-bedroom cottage on the grid power. You have to BYO partner; it is quite empty out there. It's almost the same as working the cattle stations though. We just have more quid in our pockets, Richard and me, and we earn pensions being boundary riders.

"How long have you been doing this?"

"Five years for me, Richard is three. I'm thinking of moving on though. I've put in for a promotion. The Wild Dog Destruction Board is looking for a leading hand, the second in charge. It pays $37,281."

"Well good luck with that."

"Thanks. And it will allow me to stay in a place longer. What I'm looking to do is open up a wildlife rehabilitation center for 'roos and other animals that need medical help."

Another animal person. At least I'm consistent with the men I'm attracted to, Jen thought.

Chapter 6

Sydney to Gatton

As the 747 circled Sydney Airport waiting its turn to land, the loudspeaker crackled to life.

"We are on our final approach to land in Sydney. Please follow the seat belt signs, return the seats to their original upright positions and turn off all electronic devices. On behalf of the flight crew, Qantas Airlines thanks you for flying with us. We hope you have a pleasant rest of your trip."

"We can take you north with us Jen," Brolga offered. He was hoping they wouldn't have to split up.

"We'll talk in luggage pickup, Brolga. I should get back to my assigned seat. You too."

She looked at the time. It was 9:30 in the morning, the sun was bright, and the sky was cloudless.

After disembarking she went to the counter to find out where her dog was. As she thought, things were handled automatically from here on out. She realized she had nothing to do but wait until visiting hours at the quarantine station. Brolga found her, and they walked together to baggage pickup.

"We can take you to Gatton, Jen. It's somewhat out of our way but I talked to Richard, and he is okay with you coming along."

"I appreciate that Brolga, but things are unsettled with Pounder right now. I didn't fly here to leave him alone. I'll have to pass on your offer."

A frown of disappointment flashed briefly across his face. "Well here let me give you my numbers. It would be great to meet up with you again here in Oz or maybe even back in California."

"Maybe so. Thank you for everything. You've made the trip fun." She smiled and grabbed his hand as they finished their walk to the luggage pickup.

"Well, let us take you to your hotel."

"No, I can't impose anymore."

"Yes, you can."

"Nope, I'm renting a car. It's reserved here at the Sydney Airport."

"Very well then." He gave up throwing offers her way. They talked quietly as they stood in line waiting for luggage, and then again as they waited to go through customs.

Finally, the three friends hugged and went their separate ways. Jen found the car rental kiosk and made her way to the hotel. It was close to the Eastern Creek Quarantine Station, a few miles west of Sydney.

Jen was not permitted to visit Pounder until the next day. Visiting hours were restricted to Tuesdays and Thursdays between 1:30 pm and 3:30 pm. She stayed in Sydney through two visits until she knew Pounder was happy and well cared for. Now she needed to figure out something to do for the next four days until next Tuesday. She knew herself; the wait was going to prove tedious and unbearable. Not used to sitting around, Jen called Billy.

"Mr. Billy O'Rourke?"

"This is Billy."

"Hi, this is Jen Bianchi, Billy. I've landed in Sydney and Pounder is now officially in Australian quarantine. Everything seems well organized at the station but visiting hours are severely limited. I'm going to take a motor trip and was hoping you might be able to put me up while Pounder finishes quarantine."

She felt a hesitation. "That's a surprise," he replied, after a moment. "I had not anticipated that."

"I'm sorry if I'm imposing. I can go elsewhere. I have the phone numbers of others I can visit."

"You're not imposing. I'm not used to company, Jen," he confessed. "You should come up right away; we have a place for you."

"Thank you," she gushed. She had not made plans for things to do during Pounder's quarantine. Suddenly, she felt great angst over the entire situation and Billy's acceptance of her company came as a big relief.

After her call to Billy, Jen called Randy She'd been angry with him for the longest time, but now it was time to talk. It was 11:00 in the evening in California and Randy was near the phone.

"Hey, babe! How's it going?" he asked when he heard her voice. He had been staying away from her ever since their last argument.

"This is bullshit, Randy!" She exploded over the phone.

"What is bullshit?"

"Oh, the way you're so fucking happy when I call from far away. You couldn't even find time to see me off, you, and your goddamn doctor appointments. And when I do call you, all I get is: 'Hey babe how's it going?'"

"Calm down, Jen. You know I needed that appointment. We agreed earlier that Janie would take you. But now you're angry at me." His mind went to another of his patent bromides, the things he told others when they needed an answer. He had been hiding from Jen for three weeks because he did not want her to see the extent of the injuries he sustained to his hand. He couldn't explain them without a lot of questions from Jen, and he wasn't ready to tell her where he'd been and what he was doing.

"I can book a flight and leave as soon as possible if you need me," he lied.

He couldn't have gone anyway; she hid his passport. "No, I'm a big girl. I can do this. I need you to commit to us, Randy I'd as soon stay here in Australia, as come home to a jerk like you."

"So, you flew halfway around the world to tell me this?"

"Fuck you. You need to decide if you want to continue this marriage."

"Okay truce. I'm willing. What next?"

"I'll find you when I'm ready. Goodbye, Randy"

Billy told Jen the drive from Sydney to Gatton was twelve hours. She piled her suitcases into her Ford Taurus rental car and started the engine. Jen needed to continually remind herself to drive on the wrong side of the road. Australia was not as familiar as she thought it would be. The most obvious thing was the steering wheel in the car. It was on the wrong side, and people drove on the wrong side of the road. That meant she would have to remain alert and attentive the whole way.

She headed north on Hwy 1.

The traffic out of Sydney was horrific, similar to LA during rush hour. She drove a half hour to get through Sydney's suburbs and another hour before leaving the influence of the city.

"This is like southern California along PCH," she mumbled to herself. As she turned away from the ocean onto the New England Highway the land gradually rose in elevation. She was traveling through Branxton when she saw a road sign urging motorists to **Drive Carefully. We have two cemeteries. No hospital**. Branxton was at the lower end of Hunter Valley, and the topography here was quite similar to that in the Paso Robles area. The rolling hills had been denuded of their native eucalypts many years earlier and replaced with acres and acres of vineyards. She could see horses grazing in large pastures. These were thoroughbred horse breeding ranches, each with a racetrack, broke the monotony of the vineyards

The towns became smaller as Jen left the Hunter Valley and ascended into the mountains of the Great Dividing Range. These mountains, the Eastern Highlands, make up Australia's largest mountains. Their massiveness causes lots of rain as clouds move west over them, making this region Australia's biggest watershed. She continued her drive upward along the New England Highway through a rocky landscape with deeply forested hills.

Time passed as the kilometers wore on. Jen became fatigued from reiterating over and over.... "Always stay on the left." Each time she entered a new road she reminded herself to turn into the correct lane of traffic.

Driving through the small burg of Moonby, Jen became hungry and pulled into a service station next to a statue of a giant chicken. "Is there a place I can find dinner?" she asked a local fellow at the road station.

The easygoing man laughed but shook his head. "Moonby is here mostly for the chickens, ma'am. We have four hundred people but a hundred times that many chickens. The closest food is back a few clicks in Tamworth."

She chuckled in spite of her tiredness, appreciating the Aussie's sense of humor. Returning to her car, she opened the car door on the left side. "Goddamn it!" Slamming the door closed, she entered the right side of the car and began the drive to find food and bed.

The next morning Jen continued ascending the tablelands of the Dividing Range. At Glenn Innes, she stopped for a potty break. The wind was fierce. She was at the summit of the Range. The towns reminded her of Steamboat Springs, Vail, and Aspen, Colorado, all main street wild-west towns. Soon she crossed the state line from New South Wales into Queensland and started down the mountain.

The topography tamed as the elevation dropped. The large stone outcroppings fell away to reveal broad valleys of rolling pastoral countryside. It was greener here because of the rich volcanic soil. She knew she was close to Billy's place now and called him at her next gas stop to get directions to his ranch.

Chapter 7

Billy O'Rouke's Station

"Billy this is Jen. I'm leaving Allora."

"Keep driving through Allora then take the Gatton By-Pass and drive until you see Gatton-Esk Rd. on the left. Head north a few kilometers until you see my sign, the O'Rourke Creek Station."

"What do you mean when you tell me to look for a station? Is there a gas station I need to find?" Jen asked.

"Bloody hell!" Billy exclaimed. "A place to buy gas is called a servo. A station is where we live, where we farm lucerne and raise cattle. In other words, it's a farm, a ranch, you Drongo."

Ignoring his rudeness, Jen ended the conversation and returned to the car. She turned north on the Gatton By-Pass and drove another thirty minutes. The flat valley transformed into gently rolling hills. Turning left off the main road; she spotted his sign, turned, and rumbled over a cattle grid following a dirt road a half a kilometer until she came upon two houses. The one on her right was the bigger, older one; a large two-story weatherboard house painted in white with a bull nosed veranda that extended all the way around. The more modest house was also of white weatherboard with a smaller front veranda. Both had corrugated metal roofs.

Parking in front of the larger homestead, she turned the ignition off and opened the door to three yapping Queensland Heelers. They wagged their tails in excitement; they didn't see visitors very often.

A tall man with a wiry, muscular build came out of the smaller house. He was wearing an Acubra hat. When he removed it, Jen could see his curly, strawberry blonde hair was a lot lighter in color than his beard.

Billy came up to Jen smiling. He had a strong handshake, Jen almost winced. "G'day! How ya going?" he asked.

"I'm fine but tired," Jen replied. She was frazzled and exhausted by the long road trip she began two days ago.

"Which way did you come?" Billy asked.

"I took Star Route 95 through Toowoomba."

"That's the wrong way!" Billy exclaimed. "If you had taken Hwy 15 you would have been here a half hour earlier."

Jen's fatigue made her irritated at this remark. "What does it matter to you, which way I went?" she asked. "It wasn't you who wasted a goddamn half hour!"

"No worries," Billy hastily replied trying to make up for his gaffe. "Let me get your luggage. Here, give us yer car key, I'll get ya luggage out of the boot."

"Thank you."

Walking to the trunk, he pulled out her suitcases. "Folla me," he said. "I'll show you about."

He carried the suitcases inside the smaller house and showed Jen to the guest room. "Here's your room and here is the loo," he pointed to the bathroom. "Mum is fixing dinner for everyone tonight. You needn't dress cute, just comfortable. I'll leave you to it for a while."

Jen was exhausted. She had no appetite right now and needed to be left alone. She flopped onto the bed and fell asleep.

Later, a knock woke her.

"Hello," she said. It took her a minute to remember where she was.

"We're ready for dinner!" Billy announced.

"I'll be right over," Jen replied. She changed into fresh clothes and walked across the driveway to the main house. When she was halfway there, the dogs appeared again and milled around her, wagging and barking.

Billy came charging out the front door.

"Bloody hell you lot lay down!" Billy yelled. "Sit down I, said!"

"Oh, they're okay," Jen said. "These must be your Heelers!" She crouched down and let the dogs swarm around her. They were tight-muscled, mottled colored, and very friendly dogs.

"Yes, they're Queensland Heelers," Billy replied. "They're the best workers on this station. Couldn't run the place without 'em."

Jen patted each of them, and they quieted down shrinking into the background. She walked up the painted wooden steps of the veranda to the main house.

As she entered, she felt like she'd taken a step back in time.

The ceilings were ten feet high, and the floors were varnished wood, darkened over the last hundred years.

Opposite the front door was a wooden staircase with banisters on either side. To the right of the staircase stood a large red telephone box.

"Is that from England?" she asked.

"Yep, Dad bought it for mum from an antique house in Brisbane. The phone works," he added proudly.

Jen noticed all of the furniture was huge. The sideboard along the wall, the coffee table, and the sofa were some of the largest she had ever seen. Billy took her upstairs where three bedrooms surrounded a central bathroom. The beds were huge four posters. Wooden chests were at the foot of each bed and dark, wooden armoires stood against the walls. There were animal pelts lying at the foot of the beds and draped across the chests.

"What is that fur?" she asked.

"Oh, those are 'roo and koala furs grandfather collected through the years."

Jen was horrified. "Are you allowed to hunt koala bears?" she asked.

"No, but our situation allowed us to be exempted!" replied Billy winking his right eye.

"How so?"

"Because Grandfather killed those animals, years ago so they were 'grandfathered' in." He laughed at his joke.

Nell, Billy's mum, called up the stairs to tell them dinner was ready. It was a simple affair of pork chops, mashed potatoes, cabbage, and carrots.

Already sitting at the table was Billy's dad, Ian. Ian was over eighty years old. He was feeble and moved slowly, but he had a quick mind and was an avid reader.

They ate in silence for a while and then Jen asked: "Where's your son, Billy?"

"Mick? He's probably at the pub in Gatton with his ratbag friends looking for moisties," Billy replied.

"I see." Jen paused a moment trying to decide if she should ask what 'moisties' were. "Where is Mrs. O'Rourke?"

Billy swallowed his food, pursed his lips, and scowled. He wiped his mouth with his napkin and glared at Jen. "She's gone!"

Billy's mother hurriedly rose from the table and began clearing dishes.

Jen persisted. "Gone where?"

Billy stared at Jen with an icy look. "Damn sheila! Don't you have any manners for Christ's sake? I don't want to talk about this!" He threw his napkin on the table, stood up, and angrily paced the length of the dining room. And then he yelled again. "If her story makes me uncomfortable to tell then it sure as hell will make you uncomfortable to hear!"

Billy's rage unnerved Jen. She thanked Mum for dinner and said goodnight to Ian. Excusing herself she walked to her room in the house next door, far away from the noisy, irritating, rude man.

Chapter 8

Jen's Bathtub Soak

Jen filled the bathtub with steamy hot water and began a long contemplative soak. She was half a world away from her family and pets, having immersed herself into the world of old-fashioned Australia. She was the guest of a man who was rude, arrogant, self-centered, and had anger issues.

After the tub, Jen went directly to bed. She was bone tired. Sending her cherished puppy into a thirty-day quarantine, after having spent over fourteen hours on an airplane traveling through six different time zones, and then driving on the wrong side of the road for two days had wiped her out.

She slept soundly and woke refreshed. Drawn to the light, she swung her feet to the floor facing the curtained window. Pushing it away she realized the sun was up. It was probably; about nine o'clock, late by Jen's standards. When she walked to the bathroom she noticed someone had slipped a note under the door. It was from Nell; she wanted her to come over for coffee.

Jen dressed and left her room. She was the only person in the small house. Walking to the front door, she stepped out onto the porch and was immediately overcome by a heavy, acrid fragrance in the warm, humid air. The smell came from the gum trees, eucalypts of the Australian forest that surrounded the farm.

A constant murmur of noise wafted from the forest as hundreds of birds made the gum trees their home and hangout place. The low-grade murmur was punctuated by the sharp call of other birds. Occasionally a sharp, staccato noise that sounded like a monkey laughing would emanate from the trees.

Jen made her way across the drive to see what Nell was doing. Opening the front door of the big house she walked to the kitchen where Nell was cleaning up from lunch.

"Hello dear," Nell said. "Do you want a coffee? We usually drink tea, but I have some coffee too."

"Sure, coffee would be great."

"How are you dealing with things?"

"Why do you ask?"

"Oh, because you seem to be impatient with Billy."

"I'm just not used to someone so gruff."

"Please, sit here awhile so I can tell you a story." Nell placed a steaming coffee cup in front of Jen and proceeded on.

"When Billy was a teenager, he was wild. He was a roughneck, a real Aussie male with a roving eye and a way with the ladies. Then he met Holly at the University of Queensland here in Gatton. She was studying to be an animal technician. Billy fell madly in love with her. After she graduated, she took a job with an equine practitioner in Hendra, north of Brisbane, but they continued to see each other. Billy would bring her around and show her off to dad and me and anyone else present. But his reputation still got in the way. Even after he was married, there were rumors of illicit liaisons although none were true. His love for Holly was one he never felt before."

Nell went on. "Holly quit her technician job when they married, and they moved into the house where you are staying. Mick was born less than a year later. Everything was going well. They were very happy, and they loved their boy. Then one day Holly received a call from her former veterinary employer for whom she had great respect. He needed backup help and asked Holly to come to Hendra for a few days."

Nell refilled Jen's coffee. "This veterinarian saw things in horses that he had not seen before. He needed help collecting samples to figure out what was going on. Holly fully believed in this fellow and drove over to see what she could offer. She helped the Doctor out for three days. Not long after she came home, she became sick, like she had the flu. Her vomiting became so severe we brought her to the hospital. A day later she died in spite of what they could do for her. We found out later that the vet Holly was working with became sick and died too. The hospital laboratory told us they both died from some virus that had infected their brains."

Nell took a deep breath and began the next part of the story. "When Holly died, Billy's whole world collapsed. He felt he would never be able to find a person like her to fill his world with the love they cherished. He continued with everyday activities and threw himself into working this station and raising his son. But it seemed he lost the extra drive that used to push him forward. Now Billy has found a comfortable, safe place, being by himself. And that's how he has survived the last twenty years."

"That's a shame. I'm sorry," Jen said.

"But that wasn't the end of the mess honey," Nell continued. "The authorities came in and pushed us around. They showed us court orders allowing them to take blood samples from our horses. They came in space suits. The veterinarian in charge, Dr. Bob, came from the veterinary school in Gatton. Birds were his specialty, and those people who make decisions on their own decided it was a disease being spread by birds. Dr. Bob told us we could very well be in danger of dying from something he couldn't explain. These people had space suits on." She repeated.

"Two different times this group came onto our property to look at the horses and take their blood. Losing Holly overwhelmed Billy, and now his farm was being overrun by scientists with space suits. But, we didn't die!" Nell's gaze turned inward.

Realizing they were done Jen thanked Nell for the coffee. Returning to her room, she remained undecided over Billy. She didn't know how much of Billy's outbursts were because he was a spoiled, arrogant asshole or because he felt a deep loss. But it didn't matter. Jen was here to deliver a dog and then she was going back home, back to her comfort zone.

Nell was nearing 75 years old. She was a healthy woman with steel gray hair sprinkled with white. A tad above five feet tall, with ruddy cheeks and quick, clear blue eyes, she seemed to be busy with something all the time. She was comfortable at this point in her life and proud she and Ian had not been overly meddlesome in the lives of their two children Billy and Carrie. She was also proud of the fact she helped Billy raise Mick after Holly died. Concerned about Billy and Jen, she took Billy aside the morning after talking with Jen.

"Billy, you invited this woman to stay here. Don't be mean to her. Show her around and be a host instead of a jerk."

"Oh, she's a sensitive one, is she?" Billy said.

"That's what I'm talking about, Billy," Nell scolded.

"Oh alright, Mum. I'll be nice to her."

Billy gave Nell a smile that always mollified her and Nell wondered if he could be 'nice' anymore.

Chapter 9

Australian Bats

Jen woke to a persistent tap on her door.

"I've scheduled a horseback ride today Jen. You and I are going to check the fence and water lines," Billy said through the closed door.

"That sounds great, but I'm going to need food."

"It's too late for breakfast. Besides, I fancy a bushman's breakfast, a morning piss, a good look round, and nothing to eat until lunch. I'll be waitin' outside."

"Well lunch then," she replied, as she heard his footsteps withdraw. It was amazing how fucking irritating Billy could be. She pulled on some loose-fitting jeans and laced up her sneakers.

"Good morning," she said when she opened the front door. He was waiting on the small front porch for her.

"G'day," he replied scanning her from head to toe. "We're going riding; you can't wear runners, you need riding boots. Oh, and no anal floss."

"What is anal floss?"

"Skimpy underwear that shouldn't be worn by ladies riding horses. I think you call them G-strings."

"I didn't bring my boots with me because I didn't know we would be riding horses," she retorted.

"Excuse me," Billy mumbled more words as he pushed by and went back into the small house. Soon he came out with a pair of brown, scuffed boots with spurs attached to them.

"Here, use these." He shoved them at her.

Sitting on an outside chair, Jen unlaced her shoes and put the boots on. Although they fit well, she was uneasy putting her feet into someone else's footwear. She wondered if they were Holly's but thought it best not to ask.

She followed Billy to the barn where they collected two horses for the ride. Billy saddled a bay colored thoroughbred, Dharma, for himself. He next pulled out a painted quarter horse, Babe, for Jen to ride. Billy picked the feet up on each horse and used a hoof pick to clean out any stones. Saddling them both, he put bridles on them and asked Jen if she needed help.

"No thanks," she said deftly hoisting herself into the saddle.

As they started their ride, the dogs became excited; they were going on a mission. The three Queensland Heelers, Pearl, Cecil, and Freckles wound their way among the horses yipping and barking their intention to become the meanest and most badass dogs in the neighborhood.

The ride had no goal despite what Billy said. There were no fences to mend, no escaped cattle, and no water lines needed fixing. Stray wild pigs had not compromised the lucerne fields. Once in a while, the dogs would run after a laggard cow straying from the herd, but in the end, the ride was a time for Billy and Jen to talk.

Jen was uncomfortable in the warm, humid climate but soon forgot it in the newness of this strange land. The air was scented with eucalyptus oil, and she heard a constant murmur of sounds from the trees. The cicadas were deafening at times, and then, as if a switch was suddenly turned, they would stop. Amazing. Then, Jen heard loud "kawhoo" noises continuing in groups of six or eight calls one after another

"What is that noise?"

"It's a Koel, a black cuckoo bird, with blood-red eyes," Billy replied. "It lays one single egg in another bird's nest, and the baby cuckoo gradually kills the other mates in the clutch."

Suddenly a new noise erupted. Jen heard this same sound yesterday. It was a rapid-fire staccato that reminded her of monkeys in Tarzan movies. "And what is that?" she asked Billy.

"That's a kookaburra," Billy replied. "We also call it the Laughing Jackass."

"Oh, I learned the Kookaburra song when I was in girl scouts!" Jen proclaimed, and she began singing: "Kookaburra sits in the old gum tree. Merry, merry king of the bush is he. Laugh Kookaburra! Laugh Kookaburra! Gay your life must be."

Billy laughed. "Looks as though there's a bit of Aussie in you after all."

Moving their horses, closer to the edge of the bush, Jen could make out dark shapes hanging from the trees. "I didn't know eucalyptus trees had fruit like that."

"It's not fruit; those are flying foxes, bats. They roost in the gum trees during the daylight and forage during the darkness eating fruit, pollen, and nectar from the gums."

"Our bats eat insects. They track down insects with sonar."

"Fruit bats don't need fancy radar devices; they're after fruit, not bugs," he chuckled. "The bats evolved eating the flowers from the gums. Now they eat fruit from the orchard trees planted in place of the gums. They are rather, clumsy; they aren't the stealthy silent winged insectivores that populate the other parts of the world. And they can't land worth a shit; they sort of crash land into the trees."

Suddenly Babe stopped, jolting Jen forward in her saddle. Babe was reacting to something on the ground in front of her, dancing sideways, and making efforts to turn and run home. Responding accordingly Jen dropped lower into her saddle, dipping her heels to get a better feel for her center.

Billy spied an Eastern Brown Snake that had been interrupted and irritated by the movement of the horses.

"Get away from the snake!" He yelled. "It can kill the horse."

Jen looked down to see a slender, five-foot long, greenish brown snake hissing at them. Billy pulled a shotgun from a saddle holster on his horse, took aim, and dispatched the thing with one shotgun blast.

Both horses were still unnerved, scared more by the snake than the sudden loud noise of the gun. Billy pulled on Dharma's reins while Jen did the same to get Babe under control.

As the snake was writhing in death, Jen asked Billy if it was time to go back. Billy was hesitant to answer. Evidently, he was shaken by the episode as well. He reloaded his shotgun and replaced it in the saddle holster.

"Nah... There's still plenty of time. A snake in the grass is no reason to run home."

They rode on in silence.

"Y'know you did some pretty good balancing on top of Babe as she was dancin' and spinnin'," Billy said.

"I love to ride and do it often," Jen proudly replied. The silences were uncomfortable to her, so she tried to keep the conversation going by asking another question. "Are Australian bats marsupials?"

"Oh no. Kangaroos are marsupials, bats are not," Billy answered. "Because of Australia's million-year isolation, the warm-blooded animals that developed here were marsupials. They developed an external nurturing system for their youngsters."

"Mammals have that too, that's what breasts are for."

"Kangaroo knockers are much smaller to feed the tiny babies. When these youngsters are born, they are very undeveloped, about the size of a peanut. They need a protective place to be nurtured and to grow. That's what the pouch is for. And nipples in the pouch allow the blind youngsters nourishment," Billy said.

She listened, nodding her head.

He continued. "Some of the better-known marsupials in Australia include the kangaroos, the koala bears, and the wombats. The only non-marsupial mammals before British colonization were the bats and the dingoes. These were animals from the old world, and they are called placental mammals."

"Well then," Jen pondered out loud "Where did bats and dingoes come from?"

"They made their way down the Indonesian archipelago. The first dingo to set foot in Australia likely came from the boat of a fisherman living in one of the numerous islands north of Australia in the Torres Strait. Bats didn't need boats because they can fly south from the islands of New Guinea."

Jen felt Billy was opening up; he did have a softer side. Like most men, the trick was to get him to talk about himself. She asked him about his Queensland Heelers.

"They are the Australian cattle dog," he replied. "The breed came into existence when a bloke down in New South Wales mated his family dog to a tame dingo. They do well at herding cattle, running up behind the cow and biting at the legs to make the animals go where they want," Billy continued. "However, they are clueless about retrieving, and that is why I need a Chesapeake Retriever here. What made you decide to start raising Chessies, Jen?"

"A friend of mine asked me to accompany her to a field trial for retrieving dogs," Jen explained. "She raised Chesapeake Bay Retrievers, and her dogs were the hardest working at the event. I really liked them and decided I wanted to breed them myself. I bought a puppy from my friend and began taking the dog to field trials as well as AKC events. Eventually he earned enough AKC points to be advertised as a champion. That's how I made my name in the Chessie breeding business."

Jen continued: "AKC championships are earned by entering a dog, catching the judges' eye, and slowly working your way up through the ranks. However, the most fun I have is in the field trials. Instead of the "Pomp and Circumstance" bullshit that occurs during the AKC shows the dogs in the field test events do what they want. They are not asked to walk in a ring while a judge decides that the dog's hair is wrong, or the legs or head stance aren't right. At these field trials, it is all about energy and focus and performance. They get to perform in the field instead of prancing around the ring. You can see how excited they are when you ask them to go on a retrieve; it's more fun for both the dog and the handler."

"I'm anxious to see our new pup," Billy said.

"I think he'll do great here Billy. I expect you will enjoy him." Jen smiled at her companion, glad that the tension seemed to have eased off. She was going to be here for another twenty days or so. This country was so different and strange, and now she felt she could look forward to learning about it and exploring it with Billy

Chapter 10

Billy's Roast

"Well, it's getting on for suppertime," Billy announced. "We'd better get home."

He turned Dharma around urging her into a trot. Jen galloped to catch up.

Once in the barn they unsaddled the horses and put the tack away. Billy brought out a large plastic bucket holding brushes; curry combs, and other gadgets for cleaning and brushing horses. Tied to rings in the wall, the horses stood quietly in the washing stations. Billy set the bucket down between them and the riders began cleaning the sweaty beasts.

Jen squirted Babe with a hose, which lifted the hairs loosening the grime. The water drizzled to the floor in gray rivulets. She bent down to retrieve a water blade, a flexible steel squeegee that pulls the water and dirt from the hair and brushed against Billy's hand as he reached into the bucket for a currycomb.

"Sorry," Jen said automatically.

"No worries," Billy replied. They finished cleaning the horses and lead them to the paddock to release them.

"I'll put up the halters and leads," Billy said. "Mum probably has dinner ready, so there's no time for a shower. Just take your boots off and come over to the kitchen."

Jen changed into her sneakers and headed to the main house. Billy was right; dinner was already on the table. Ian sat waiting next to a thin young man with dark brown hair and freckles.

"You must be Mick," Jen exclaimed.

"Yep," Mick replied as he stood up to shake Jen's hand. "G'day to you, ma'am"

"It is nice to meet you," Jen said. "I was beginning to wonder if there was a Mick around here!"

Mick smiled and chuckled. "I'm usually with my mates from the university." He saw Billy walk in with a disapproving look on his face. "But that is when there is no work to be done here!" Mick added.

They settled into places around the table, and the meal began.

As Mick sipped his second beer, he poked some fun at his father. "Y'know, Dad's never brought a woman home before." He looked at his dad mischievously.

Billy scowled, and Nell chuckled. Jen was embarrassed, and Ian didn't hear anything.

"She's not like that. Oh, I know you're a woman, just not like that," Billy said uncomfortably, letting the sentence trail off.

After a few moments of awkward silence, Nell stood up. "It's time for some dessert!"

Jen picked up plates from the table to help out and placed them in the sink. Nell lifted the cover off a beautifully decorated, aromatic chocolate cake. Jen was mightily impressed. "Oh Nell, that's beautiful. You have such talent."

"I didn't make this cake dear," Nell confessed. "I cannot find time for this fussy stuff. This one's from Stephie, one of Billy's..." she paused. Her hands made circular motions as her mind searched for the right word. Nell inhaled and continued. "I call them handmaidens."

"Billy's handmaidens?" Jen asked in total surprise.

Nodding, Nell continued with a story. "When Holly died several people brought food, you know, to help out during a hard time. Well, some of the single women in town never stopped. These women have changed over the years as they became married off, but it seems there are always one or two gifts left here each week. I even leave a cooler by the front door in case we're gone."

Nell picked up the cake to deliver it to the dining room. Jen collected dessert plates and followed her.

"Who's this one from?" Billy asked.

"This is from handmaiden Stephie darling," Nell replied with a twinkle in her eyes.

"You can't stop encouraging them, can you?" Billy proclaimed with some irritation. "She spreads the word every Sunday at church," he complained to Jen. "I have nothing to do with this stuff."

"We can't let it go to waste or sit on the porch and dry up like Miss Havisham's wedding cake!" Nell said laughing.

"Good one Grams," Mick said as he joined in the laughter.

"Don't take any notice of them!" Billy retorted. "Sometimes I feel their only entertainment is pestering me."

Once dessert was over, the men vacated the table leaving Jen and Nell to do the dishes.

"Would it be all right if I brought some flowers into the small house where I'm staying?" Jen asked.

"Of course! Flowers are to be enjoyed," Nell replied, and got a vase out of the cupboard for her.

"Thanks for dinner Nell," Jen said, when the kitchen was clean.

As Jen walked toward the front door, Nell called out from the kitchen: "Don't forget coffee with me in the morning!"

"I'll be here, goodnight Nell."

Jen went right to the bathtub and filled it with steaming hot water. Stripping her clothes off she slipped into the comfort of the warm liquid. She needed to think about things; here in the hot tub, she could sort out the confusion of the day.

Oddly, she felt herself being drawn into this family. A feeling of strength emanated from them. Or was it a power that came from the family homestead, their station? Maybe it was because this was an extended family that shared many years of success and frustration together. She decided much of the family integrity came from Nell's evenness and steadfastness. *She is the glue that holds everything together,* Jen thought.

But what will happen when Nell is gone? She wondered. Billy had been running away from women for twenty plus years. Nell had mentioned a daughter, Carrie who did not seem interested in the family events. Mick was way too young to run a station. Ian was too old to be any influence at all. "Oh well, I am simply a temporary visitor, and I need to remember that," Jen told herself as she dried off, put pajamas on, and slid into bed. She immediately fell into a deep sleep.

The next morning Jen dressed remembering Nell's invitation. As she walked through Billy's kitchen, she saw the empty vase Nell gave her the night before. She went into the garden, clipped half a dozen blossoms, and set them on the table. Then she ran over to see Nell. She found her in the kitchen cleaning up from breakfast.

"Where did the boys go?" Jen asked.

"They're out by the paddocks. It's time for another cutting and Billy needs Mick's help working the equipment."

"Do you have time for coffee with me?" Jen asked.

"Certainly dear."

As Jen was sipping her coffee, Nell said: "You seem to have made quite an impression on Billy."

"What makes you think that Nell?"

"Because he is less grumpy than usual. He usually acts like he is wearing a stone around his neck. You actually make him smile."

Jen panicked. "Nell," she murmured. "I don't know if Billy told you, but I'm married."

The words unnerved Nell who immediately backtracked on her assumption. "Billy never told me that. I apologize if the things I have been saying are making you uncomfortable."

"No, there is nothing for you to apologize for Nell. I appreciate your hospitality and am very impressed with how you run this station. I think you are the glue that holds everything together."

Flustered in embarrassment, Nell waved her hand dismissively.

"I mean it, Nell. I am very grateful you have agreed to let me stay with you during the quarantine period. This is a lot more fun than sitting in a hotel room in Sydney waiting to see Pounder on Tuesday and Thursday afternoons."

"I'm glad we are able to accommodate you, my dear."

They talked for a short while longer until Nell was antsy to get back to her chores. Jen thanked her for the coffee and returned to the smaller house. She tidied up her room and made her way to the kitchen. Adjusting the flowers in their vase, she looked around and decided on a way she could show her gratitude to her hosts. She would paint the walls in the smaller house. They looked like they hadn't been painted for years. She walked back to tell Nell of the idea. "I'll get Billy to take you to the paint shop later today!" Nell exclaimed.

Jen was excited as well. She was never one for sitting around, and now she had a project she could focus her energy on.

Chapter 11

Paint Wars

When Billy returned home, Nell approached him carefully. "Billy, Jen has offered to do some painting in the little house."

"Painting? Painting what?" Billy sputtered.

"Well, the kitchen and the dining room. They haven't been painted for years, and they're in great need of a pick-me-up. You can choose the color dear. I wanted to do the project myself, but I have so much else to do, and I'm not good on a ladder anymore. I think that it is wonderful for Jen to offer." Nell kept on talking not giving Billy a chance to interrupt. "You must go now. You have enough time to get to the paint store before dinner."

Billy knew it was no use arguing with Nell when she was like this. He stomped out of the house. After slamming the car door hard, he honked the horn impatiently for Jen.

She came inquisitively to the kitchen door.

"Get in," he yelled. "We've got to get to the paint store before dinner."

As Jen went to the car, she started towards the driver's side, but corrected herself and opened the passenger door.

"Still not used to it, eh Jen?" Billy asked.

"Old habits die hard," she replied. They drove down the driveway in silence, almost. Billy was grumbling under his breath.

Jen ignored the grumbling for a bit and then questioned Billy. "What are you percolating about over there?"

"I don't see why we have to go through the expense and trouble of painting! Those walls have been fine for twenty years."

"Billy it's only a small expense. I'll pay for the paint if that's the problem."

"You're not paying for anything! This is my house. It's my paint!"

"And you'll choose the color," interrupted Jen. "I am the one who is going to be painting. The walls need it, and I need something to do while I am here. If it is that much of a problem, then turn around right now. We'll go back to your grungy little house, and no more will be said! I'm sorry, but you are such a grump."

Jen turned away from him looking out the window, watching the beautiful Queensland countryside go by. Once again, she was struck by the greenness of it. Central California had a brief season of green in the spring, but this was downright tropical.

Billy didn't turn the car around. He cleared his throat and said: "So you've got a little temper, eh?"

Jen didn't respond. If she said what she was thinking it would have started the argument up all over again likely sending someone to the hospital.

More silence.

"So, tell me of the pup," Billy began again.

This was something Jen always and forever wanted to share. "Well, he is a tannish color; we call it 'dead grass.' He is a good-sized puppy with a great personality. He's happy and energetic, but not too hyper and he loves people. I feel he is quite bright and is eager to please. He should be easy to train.

"Did you name him yet?" Billy asked.

"He has a litter name, Pounder, but you'll have to give him his registered name.

"Pounder! That's an unusual name."

"We called him that because he pounds the ground with his front paws when he gets excited. We give them litter names, so we can identify them. He doesn't answer to it yet, so you can change the name to whatever you want."

"Pounder sounds great to me," Billy exclaimed. "But he's Mick's pup, so it will be up to him."

51

"We start training our dogs before they leave our home," Jen continued, "so he knows not to jump up, and he knows to stop barking when you command, and he is somewhat house trained."

"House trained?" Billy asked.

"Yes, he has been trained to pottie on papers in the house, and he's learning to hold it for outside."

"Well we won't have to worry about that," Billy replied. "Our dogs never come inside."

"Chessies need to be inside Billy. They need to be part of the human family and close to their alpha dog which will be whoever trains him, Mick probably."

"Well, we can talk about that later," Billy said.

Things quieted for a while and Jen changed the subject. "Why are Australians so afraid of rabies?" She asked.

"Australians are NOT afraid!" Billy replied exasperatedly.

Jen backtracked and tried a different approach although she couldn't hide the irritation in her voice. "What I meant is that other countries have rabies and the people seem to be doing okay with it. What makes rabies such a dire consequence if it enters Australia?"

Billy didn't answer her. They had talked enough. He pulled into the lot at the paint store and exited the vehicle. Jen opened her car door and hurried to follow him inside. She walked to the color wall and started pulling out color samples.

"What is your favorite color, Billy? Do you want the rooms to all be the same color? Do you like dark colors or pastels?"

Billy was quiet for a while and then said, "White. I want white walls white ceilings. White is fine."

"White it is then," replied Jen. They chose a shiny finish for the kitchen and a matte finish for the other rooms as well as paintbrushes and some other supplies. By the time they returned to the station dinner was on the table. After dinner, Jen helped Nell cleanup then went straight to bed. She would start her painting project first thing in the morning.

By late afternoon of the next day, Jen was tired, having spent the entire day washing the kitchen and dining room walls; she was ready to begin painting. Stopping by the big house for a snack she told Nell she was going to bed early and wouldn't be there for dinner.

Jen filled her bathtub with another batch of steamy, welcoming water, reflecting on the strengths of this family as she slid into the warmth. They were living on property they owned and farmed for five generations. Billy and Mick worked the station, and Nell was the homemaker who added another link to the chain. Obviously, they didn't get along all the time, but she felt they had a deep love and trust for each other. Jen wanted to foster those feelings in her own family.

Over the years she had been married to Randy, she had allowed an emotional distance to separate them. Sadly, and possibly too late, she realized she had not tended to her marriage. She and Randy were more like aloof friends than close lovers. Being presented with such family closeness here at the station made Jen yearn for the same feeling back home. *I'll just have to work at it and make it happen,* she told herself. *I can do this. I can do anything I set my mind to.*

She went to bed satisfied with the new course she had set for herself.

Chapter 12

Carrie Comes to Visit

The next morning was a bright, sunny Saturday. When Jen walked into Nell's kitchen she noticed Nell was unusually busy.

"What's the fuss about?"

"Our daughter Carrie, Billy's sister, is coming over from Brisbane for the weekend!" Nell exclaimed excitedly.

"Oh, that's great! I'll get to meet her," Jen said.

"Mick's coming too; he's already here. He came in last night. He's helping Billy check fence lines."

"What does Carrie do in Brisbane?" Jen asked.

"She works for a veterinary distribution company. She goes around to various veterinarians to sell them drugs and supplies."

Jen and Nell worked together on a meal of homemade bread and pot roast with boiled potatoes and carrots that came from Nell's garden. Midway through the afternoon, a small compact car drove up the dusty driveway. The three dogs circled the car barking their excitement. An attractive woman emerged and made her way directly to the big house. She was tall and slender with the same wiry build as Billy. Her hair was a darker red and there was a lot of it. It blew around her head in the wind, which made her look like a fiery goddess. She had a confident stride and a warm smile.

Jen and Nell walked out on the front porch to greet her. "Hi, Mum!" Carrie said as she hugged Nell. "And who's this?"

"This is a friend of Billy's," Nell replied. "Jen, this is Billy's sister, Carrie. Carrie this is Jen.

"A *friend* of Billy's, you say!" Carrie asked with a grin.

"Yes, a friend Carrie. Jen brought a puppy to Australia. Billy's buying it from her, but it has to spend four weeks in quarantine in Sydney. So, Billy invited her up to spend some time with us."

"Hello, Carrie," Jen said. "It's nice to meet you."

"Oh, you're American!" Carrie said excitedly. "Are you staying here the entire time? I want to pick your brain about that beautiful country. You'll have to come and stay with me in Brisbane because you'll go crazy out here after a while."

"Oh, I would love that!" said Jen. "I want to know more of Australia as well!"

As they entered the house, Carrie said, "Umm smells good. What's for dinner?"

She pitched in to help finish dinner preparations. Soon the table was set, and the family seated themselves around it. Afterward, Nell brought out an apple pie dropped off by another hopeful neighbor and served ice cream alongside.

The girls brought the dishes into the kitchen and Carrie announced she and Jen were going to sit outside on the porch to enjoy the summer evening as soon as the dishes were cleaned.

"Leave them, I'll do them tomorrow," Jen said.

But Nell couldn't allow dishes in the sink to stay dirty. "As grandmother used to say, 'never put off until tomorrow, what you can do today'," she said, shaking her head.

The moon was full, and the animals in the bush were very active. Carrie shared a bottle of Australian Chardonnay with Jen. As they chatted, Jen realized she liked Carrie, and felt that unlike Billy, she could talk to her about anything. When Carrie asked her about the puppy, she'd brought over, Jen told her of the tests and shots Rory gave, and yet he still needed to sit in quarantine for four weeks.

"There seems to be a lot of concern over rabies in Australia," Jen said. "Why is that such a big problem?"

"We've never had rabies in Australia, Jen," Carrie said.

"Really, wow!"

"Umm-hmm, Australia's tough import requirements have successfully kept rabies out of the country. However, as the world's climate and populations are changing there is always the possibility of the virus entering virgin territory. Currently there is the threat from the Indonesian island archipelago."

"Where's that?" Jen asked.

"They are islands to the north and west of Australia. Twenty-two of the thirty-three provinces in Indonesia are experiencing a spread of the rabies virus. Five hundred kilometers north of Darwin, the island of Palau Jamdena fell to an outbreak that probably came in from a dog on a fisherman's boat. Nineteen people on that island died of rabies. Australian officials are worried rabies will jump across the Torres Strait to the Cape York Peninsula."

"Give me your worst-case scenario."

"Okay, a fisherman's boat leaves Palau Jamdena and travels south-southeast for two hundred kilometers catching lots of fish when motor problems develop, and the fellow comes aground at Garig Gunak Barlu National Park in Australia. One of the dogs on board is developing a rabies infection that hasn't blown up yet. The dog is a male not neutered of course and runs off when he scents a bitch dingo in heat. And, bingo! Rabies has been introduced into Australia. That's how easy it is."

"I never thought about a rabies epidemic before. We vaccinate our animals at four months and keep them current after that," said Jen. "Why don't you do that here?"

"It's a combination of factors," Carrie said. "The northern territories have a sparse human population and hundreds of wild dogs, dingoes. The Aboriginal tribes make up most of the population and they don't have the knowledge, organization, or finances to make vaccinations an easy option. Wait here a moment! I'll see if I can find one of Holly's old books."

She returned in a few minutes carrying a textbook on infectious diseases between people and animals.

She looked up Rabies and began a recitation: "Both North and South America were free of rabies until sometime in early 1800 when it was brought over by an infected animal from Europe. Once it came to the Americas, rabies inserted itself into the native populations of wild carnivores, dogs, skunks, coyotes, wolves, foxes, and bats. Once in these populations, it is spread through their saliva when they bite their prey."

"So, you have to be bitten to get it?" Jen asked.

"Yes," Carrie answered, "And here is what the infection does to humans." Carrie continued to read. "The virus begins reproducing in muscle cells near the bite site during the next two days. During this time of local viral replication, the bitten person feels tingling, burning, and numbness near the wound. Shortly afterward the new viruses find a nerve close to the infected muscle and travel along the nervous system until they reach the spinal cord. In people, this stage causes fever up to 102 degrees, also irritability, malaise, headache, and increasing anxiety.

Once in the spinal cord, the rabies viruses continue to move towards the brain. When it enters the brain, the infected person becomes confused, exhibits bizarre behavior, and may hallucinate. The body temperature continues to rise as high as 105 degrees. Soon after that the individual becomes abnormally sensitive to bright light, loud noises and reacts violently from others touching the skin or trying to hold the infected person's hand for comfort."

"They don't even like to be touched! How horrible."

"I know," Carrie replied. "And it gets worse. As the virus continues to replicate within the brain, damage to the brainstem occurs. Mild spasms appear in the throat muscles, the voice becomes hoarse and swallowing and breathing become harder. The throat muscles get so irritated and painful the mere sight of water evokes spasms. The combination of excessive salivation and difficulty in swallowing produces the traditional picture of foaming at the mouth.

After reproducing in the brain, the virus travels to the central nervous system along nerves connected to the salivary glands, the kidneys, the lungs, and even the muscles. The infected person becomes paralyzed and can no longer swallow. Soon the respiratory muscles of the diaphragm quit working, and the person dies because he can no longer breathe."

"Suffocation, what a horrible way to die!" Jen exclaimed as Carrie closed the book and put it on the table.

The daytime cacophony from the bush built up as darkness fell. Jen heard a continuous high-pitched yip-yip-yip coming from the blackness.

"Are those dingoes?" She asked. "We have coyotes that sound like that."

"No," Carrie told her. "That noise comes from sugar gliders. A dingo has a long moaning howl much like the wolf you have in America."

"Are sugar gliders the bats Billy and I saw in the trees yesterday?" Jen asked.

Billy came out with Mick as Jen enquired about the sugar gliders. They pulled up some chairs and popped open the beers they brought out with them. Carrie handed them a bag to throw the tops in.

"Naw," Billy answered. "The bats you saw in the trees were flying foxes. They sound like birds squawking during the day or monkeys chattering in the trees. Listen carefully, and you can hear their chatter right now. Flying foxes hang from limbs; sugar gliders build nests of leaves in tree hollows."

"Sugar gliders?" Jen asked. "What an unusual name. What do they look like?"

"They are cute little furry things that are like little squirrels," Carrie said. "They fit into the palm of a person's hand, and many people have brought them out of the wild and tamed them. Some people get quite attached," Carrie said. "I can take you to Brisbane's zoo to see them; they usually have an exhibit of them there."

"How about tomorrow?" Jen asked.

"Sure, we can go tomorrow. Even after tomorrow, my schedule is fairly open. I don't have any appointments for a few days."

"Tomorrow it is then," Jen said. "This is exciting!"

Chapter 13

Brisbane

Carrie and Jen got to know each other better on their drive to the Brisbane Zoo. "How did you learn so much about veterinary medicine Carrie?" Jen asked.

"Billie and I both attended the University of Queensland at the Gatton Campus. He received a Diploma in Agriculture, and two years later I received a Diploma in Veterinary Technology, the same year Holly did.

I was employed as a vet assistant like Holly. But when she died I was too nervous to work the hands-on environment. Nobody knew how they died and that scared me."

"I heard about Holly." Jen said.

"I was the person who introduced Holly to Billy. Remember, I told you Holly and I were in a lot of classes together studying to be animal technicians?"

"Umm hmm," Jen replied.

"When we graduated Holly took a position as a technician with a large animal veterinarian in Hendra. I went to Brisbane to work at a small animal practice. Holly and Billy dated for the next four years until both of them finally tired of the long-distance romance. Holly quit her job in Hendra when they married."

"Four years! That's a long time to be engaged," Jen exclaimed. "Can you tell me more of what happened to Holly? Your mom told me a little, but they don't seem to be comfortable talking about it."

"When Mick was four years old Holly received a call from her former employer in Hendra. He was bummed when Holly left the practice. She had been such a good tech, and they got on well. Now he had come across a problem he never saw before. He had been called out to treat a horse for colic but noted additional signs not seen with a stomach problem. This horse had a fever, her gums were yellow, and she was discharging a clear fluid from her nose, which gradually became bloody. The horse was dead the next morning. The vet asked Holly to come help with the necropsy because she was particularly talented at collecting post-mortem samples," Carrie continued.

"Three or four days after coming back home Holly fell ill. She thought she had the flu. Her muscles ached, and she developed a fever, a sore throat, and began vomiting. We brought her to the hospital in Gatton, but even with the intensive care, she died in two days. Her death devastated Billy and scared the daylights out of me. A few days later the vet died as well. That was when I quit hands-on animal work to become a veterinary distributor."

"Why haven't I heard of this before? I would think everyone should know such a virus is out there." Jen was incredulous.

"The first evidence of it was in 1994, and the episodes that followed that first event happened sporadically only once every year or two. Over time they did find out it was a new virus, but no one knew how it spread," Carrie said, slowing and turning into Brisbane's Alma Park Zoo.

"I'll pay for admission, you drove," Jen offered.

Although on a mission to introduce sugar gliders to Jen they appreciated other animals on exhibit. Carrie took her to the mammal section looking for Australian marsupials. They were standing in front of the koala habitat. "You know I always knew marsupials only came from Australia," Jen said. "I didn't realize there are no placental mammals, native here. That is so fascinating to me. It shows how completely isolated Australia was for millions of years,"

"I suppose it's a strange place to you," Carrie replied. "It never seemed odd to me until I started learning about everything else out there. We do have our own little world."

The girls enjoyed the koala exhibits. Jen saw what a Tasmanian Devil looked like and Carrie showed her the wallabies and kangaroos. They went looking for the bats, and sugar gliders but only the Spectacled Flying Fox was on display.

The Flying Foxes rested by hanging upside down like the ones Jen saw in the eucalypts. With one foot grabbing onto the netting above them they wrapped their large wings around themselves in a black shroud. Near ten inches in length, these bats were different from the ones Jen saw at Billy's. Their large eyes peered steadily at the zoo visitors.

"These bats are creepy!" Jen exclaimed. "They don't look like the ones hanging in the trees at the ranch. These are bigger and black. The ones I saw were small and red-brown."

"The ones you saw are Little Red Flying Foxes. Possibly they're too common to have at a zoo; they are the most plentiful. This is the endangered spectacled critter and is only found on a small stretch of coastal land on the eastern edge of the Cape York Peninsula. That must be why they keep them here."

"You never said how the Hendra virus spreads. Do these bats carry the virus?"

"All bats are reservoirs and capable of transmitting the virus. But so far Hendra has only been seen in eastern Queensland and northeastern New South Wales. We call that the Hendra Belt."

"What do you mean the bats are reservoirs?" Jen asked.

"The virus is happy living inside the bats. The bats don't react to it; the infection causes no harmful effects in them. It's probably been that way for eons, and now with more humans and horses pushing into the bush, the inevitable viral spillover into different species occurs. So now, with the virus in a different body, it causes deadly effects."

"Do you think the Hendra Virus thrives by infecting horses or people?"

"No, definitely not. Those are dead-end avenues, Jen. Viruses are parasites and they need another living organism to live in and draw nutrients from. If the parasite kills off its host, there won't be any more to feed on."

"Oh, I get it! It's best to steal a little cash from your boss for years instead of grabbing an entire payroll, right?"

Carrie stopped talking and looked at Jen with a surprised face. "Umm I suppose so," she said chuckling at the analogy.

The girls could not find sugar gliders anywhere, so they looked up the Head Zoo-Keeper who told them they were too common. They stayed a while longer and wandered through the primate and bird areas.

"Why don't you spend the night at my flat?" Carrie asked suddenly. "I'm less than twenty minutes away. I'll show you night time in Brisbane."

"Okay! That sounds like fun."

That evening they went to a local pub had a nice dinner, and a bit too much to drink.

The next morning Jen woke with a nagging headache. She followed the aroma of coffee to the kitchen. Carrie was already there. "Good morning Luv."

"Hello," Jen replied. With coffee and toast, Jen's head cleared. "Can you tell me more of the Hendra virus? I had nightmares about it."

"That's from having too much fun last evening," Carrie said as she sipped her coffee. Setting her cup down, she went to a file cabinet and pulled out a thick file folder. "This is a timeline of the virus I collected from lectures, journals, and newspapers over the years. Ready?"

Jen nodded.

"August 1994, two horses died within a few days in the northern Brisbane suburb of Hendra. Those two horses were the ones attended to by Holly's employer. The first horse died and the second wasn't responding to treatment. That was when the doctor called Holly out. A private laboratory said the death was due to avocado poisoning and also said the second horse died from snakebite! That's how totally in the dark we were Jen!"

"I can see that."

"A week later, both the veterinarian and Holly were in different hospitals fighting for their lives. Even though they were in intensive care, they both died.

Then one month later, news came of mysterious deaths at Vic Rail's racing stable. Vic was hospitalized and died. More horses started dying, causing a total cessation of racing activities."

"They shut the track down? Wow!"

Carrie nodded. "A total of thirteen horses were dead or were euthanized. It was during this second outbreak that samples revealed the appearance of a hitherto unknown virus. The virus was named Hendra because that was where it was first discovered. They developed a reliable test using the viral footprint and found seven horses infected at Vic's place. All positives were euthanized even if they appeared normal and healthy. We were scared shitless Jen. But then no more problems were seen until January 1999…"

"That's five years later!"

"Umm, hmm. A dead horse was diagnosed with Hendra virus in Townsville, a fifteen-hour drive north of Brisbane."

"Wow, that's far away," Jen exclaimed.

"Yes," said Carrie "and then Hendra disappeared for another five years until October 2004 in Gordonvale, a four-hour drive north of Townsville. The veterinarian who performed the necropsy on the dead horse became critically ill but survived in intensive care. Blood tests on the vet were positive for the Hendra virus. As you see it pops up here and there willy-nilly, but it is very deadly to people as well as horses.

And, there's more. In December 2004, another dead horse in Townsville tested positive for Hendra.

In June 2006, Dr. Rebekka Day was the first person to diagnose Hendra a live horse. The incident occurred in Peachester, one hour north of Brisbane.

After that, it was October 2006, when the first case of a horse dying from Hendra in New South Wales, the state south of Queensland, was documented in Murwillumbah, one and a half hours drive south of Brisbane.

In June 2007, another horse died of Hendra virus in Peachester.

August 2009, in Rockhampton, a seven-hour drive north of Brisbane along the coast, another deadly outbreak occurred which took the life of veterinarian Dr. Alister Rogers.

September 2009 saw another dead horse positive for Hendra virus in Bowen, a town five hours north of Rockhampton.

In May 2010, Hendra outbreak was found at Tewantin, a two-hour drive along the coast north of Brisbane.

In June 2010, multiple Hendra cases were found throughout Queensland.

And finally, on July 26, 2011, a dog named Dusty tested positive for the virus."

"A dog!" Jen said. "Really? It affects dogs too?"

"Yes, but the story stops here because there haven't been any new cases since then," Carrie declared gathering her papers.

"Hopefully that means that it has played itself out. But, how did they figure out bats carried it?"

"Doctors at the school of Veterinary Science of Queensland in Brisbane wondered if droppings from bats were causing this.

So, bingo, they found the virus by testing blood in 521 Spectacled Flying Foxes. They found it living in the bats!"

"And the bats don't die from the infection," Jen observed.

"Yes, it's that reservoir thing I explained earlier. Bats have a unique way of living through viral infections. They can carry the rabies virus for a long time without being killed from it, and evidently, they can carry the Hendra virus too."

"What does that mean?"

"It means the bats you saw roosting in the trees at the station could be carrying the Hendra virus."

Jen was incredulous and unnerved. "Then why aren't there programs to get this infection under control?"

"It took a few years for authorities as well as the public to get a handle on the problem because the disease was so sporadic. Many people are now criticizing the government for their lack of initial efforts. However, I think this criticism comes more easily when you are viewing the problem a few years after it happened than while it is going on."

"We call that Monday morning quarterbacking," said Jen.

"What?"

"It's a football reference. It's always easier to see what you should have done after the game is over."

"Football, oh yes that American game. I've only seen it a few times, and it is annoying."

Jen laughed. "That's exactly how I feel about soccer but people who like it get so excited."

"Yes, we do," said Carrie. "Anyways when the disease first occurred many individuals in the racing industry believed this was an isolated incident or that the disease was misdiagnosed. Because of the sporadic outbreak, as well as the five-year hiatus after 1999, racing got back to normal, and many people chose to push the problem back in their minds. The industry went on as usual, with no plan in place in case of future outbreaks," Carrie stated.

"It's like a time bomb," Jen said. "Only no one knows where it is or when it's going to go off."

"Yes," Carrie replied. "It also takes a bit of time after a problem is recognized before investigators begin to understand the epidemiology. Because the virus was never seen before, one could not go to the scientific journals for a clearer understanding.

It was not until 2000 that the virus was identified, and the information published. It also took the government sixteen years after the 1994 event, to begin allocating large sums of money to the problem. Because of bureaucratic stumbling, no official investigation into the mysterious deaths of the first handful of people who had died was conducted."

Carrie looked at the clock. It was well into the afternoon on this sunny Sunday. "I'm hungry'" she announced. "Let's go out to eat."

"It's my turn to pay," Jen insisted.

"If you don't mind, I want us to have a lavish evening!" Carrie replied.

"My wallet is open," Jen said.

After showering and dressing, Carrie called for reservations. She booked two for an evening at the Customs House.

"Oh, this is beautiful," Jen exclaimed seated on the outside terrace overlooking the Brisbane River. As darkness conquered the day and the city lights emerged she looked down on the river. Boats making their way up and down proudly shined their lights and often blared their horns. The Story Bridge to the east was beautifully lit, and Jen marveled in the majesty of the town.

"This is why I live in Brisbane!" Carrie proudly exclaimed as they ate veal scaloppini and had crème Brulee for desert.

"Before I take you back to the station tomorrow I want to introduce you to a veterinarian who has a client with sugar gliders," Carrie said on their way back to the flat.

The next morning Carrie drove Jen west towards Gatton and turned off at Hatton Vale, the township after Gatton, pulling into the lot of an equine veterinary clinic.

"Hi Doc," Carrie said shaking hands with a middle-aged woman in coveralls and muck boots who walked out of the cinderblock, one-story hospital as they drove up. "I've nothing to pitch to you today. However, I am entertaining a friend from America who wants to see sugar gliders. Also, I have told her about the Hendra virus outbreaks and she would like your opinion on some matters. Do you have time?"

"Sure. I'm heading there now for a foal check. Get in."

The three women made their way to a truck with a large white fiberglass carrier on the back. It was the doc's Vet Pak, Australian version. The truck was a double cab with four doors.

Carrie had Jen get in the front with Doc while she sat in the back seat.

"Talk to us about the Hendra virus please Doc," Carrie said.

"Hendra is a living nightmare! Vet students learn zoonotic diseases during school, but this virus is sneaky as well as deadly."

"What do you mean when you say zoonotic?" Jen asked.

"Those are diseases that can jump from animals to people."

"And what do you mean by saying this virus is a sneaky one?"

"After the first two incidents occurred in Hendra the virus disappeared again. Plus, unlike any other virus we have seen there is a direct effect on the equine practitioners as well as their technicians," Carrie said. "That is exactly why I quit working directly on animals. My anxiety levels were at an all-time high."

"It's creating an atmosphere of frustration and resentment among the equine vets in Queensland," the doctor added. "Many vets who practice on all animals have quit treating horses, and this leads to more work for the remaining ones. And some of the horse vets will only see healthy animals and refuse to deal with sick horses. That causes the other equine vets to grumble that these vets are choosing easy money over hard, dangerous money. It's quite an unpatriotic showing.

And the Queensland government is not helpful," the doctor continued. "Current legislation has declared private veterinarians are responsible for the safety of all persons in their workplace, both in the clinic and the field. Of twenty veterinary professionals queried in Queensland, seven of these vets had dealt with a confirmed case of Hendra, and four of them reported ceasing the equine practice. Veterinarians have a legal right to refuse service if they feel compromised, but this would lead to income loss as well as possibly tarnishing their reputation."

"What a crappy situation!" Jen said.

"Exactly," the doc replied. "And what makes the problem worse is the government is constantly updating the guidelines a vet must follow when approaching a suspected horse. Currently, we are told to wear splash-proof overalls with long sleeves, impervious boots, double gloves, a face shield or safety glasses, and a P2 particle respirator to prevent inhalation of aerosols.

When finished these articles need to be thoroughly disinfected or disposed of before the vet leaves the premises!"

"All that to check on a sick horse! Unbelievable!" Carrie said.

"Dr. Leighton, I have another question," Jen said. "How do the horses get the infection from bats? Do the bats bite them?"

"There doesn't have to be a bite to pass the infection. The bats only need to soil the horse's food with their secretions. Urine, feces, and fetal fluids expelled during birth contain millions of virus particles. When animals eat contaminated feed, they pull the Hendra virus into their body."

Doc Leighton pulled into a driveway and drove past a house to the barn. She greeted the owner of the new foal. "G'day!" she chirped as she jumped out of the truck. With no evidence of Hendra virus on this farm the doctor's personal protection equipment was not necessary. "Did you get a filly or a colt?"

"A filly ma'am," replied Nick O'Reilly. He attached a lead rope to mama's halter. "Delivery went fine, and I reckon you will not find any problems."

Nick had wrapped the mare's tail in a gauze wrap, which was still in place. The doctor walked to the hind end. Lifting up the horse's tail she peered inside the vagina looking for tears from the birthing process.

"No tears, and minimal bruising; it went well for her."

She moved down to the mare's udder feeling for pain, swelling, or heat. Next, she sampled milk from each nipple by pinching the tip. The fluid was slightly yellow from colostrum, which was normal. She squirted milk samples into a clean red top tube and placed it in her pocket.

"Are you going to run a culture?" Jen asked.

"Nope, I'm taking the sample to run an agglutination test alerting me in advance if the mare's colostral antibodies will kill off the baby's red cells. It's a potentially fatal and very preventable problem."

"How do you prevent it?"

"We don't let known affected mares suckle their foals until twenty-four hours have elapsed."

"What happens if you let them?"

"The milk antibodies rip the red cells apart creating anemia and jaundice. The foal turns yellow because its liver is busy recycling the broken red cells and the jaundice is a by-product of this degradation."

Finished with the mare, the doctor grabbed the foal by the tail and bent down to check the umbilical region. After seeing no problems, she placed a small cup of iodine under the foal's belly and jiggled it to cover the belly button with the disinfectant. With a stethoscope in her ears, she listened to the heart for murmurs then placed two fingers in the filly's mouth to make sure she had a good suckle reflex. Then Doc ran her fingers along the roof of the mouth to feel for a cleft palate. Finally, she pulled a syringe with a clear liquid out of her pocket and injected the newborn.

"That was tetanus antitoxin," she said.

She pulled a new, empty syringe from her pocket and drew some blood from the neck of the squirming foal.

"What is that for?" Jen asked.

"I thought you were familiar with all this," Carrie said, as she reached for her ever-present hand sanitizer bottle she carried in her handbag.

"I don't breed my horses I ride them. So, this is all new to me." She lied a bit but that was because she was in awe of Carrie. She was drawn to this strong woman and chose to keep quiet to avoid being embarrassed.

"The blood draw is the second part of the foal agglutination test," Dr. Leighton replied as she pushed the blood into a small tube with a lavender colored rubber stopper.

The doctor asked where the placenta was. She wanted to make sure the entire thing slipped out during foaling. The mare could develop a severe infection making her infertile if parts of the organ remained inside.

"In a bucket over here," Nick showed her. Pulling out the heavy afterbirth, the Doc laid it flat onto the cement to see if all the pieces were present.

"It all looks good. Congratulations!" Doc announced and gave Nick a reassuring smile. While she was washing up, she asked Nick if he would mind showing her guests his sugar gliders.

"Sure," he replied, "why wouldn't I?"

"Because I'm not entirely sure having these buggers is legal. I didn't want to put you in a hard place."

"Oh, I have a Queensland Wild Life Demonstrator License," he replied. "It allows me legal possession of the sugar gliders so long as I hold a demonstration on them at places other than my home at least once a month. The hope is to use these presentations to promote wildlife conservation. Follow me."

He led the way behind the barn where they entered a large caged area. There were six wooden nesting boxes wired to the sides of the cages about five feet from the ground. Each box had an entrance hole 1 ½" in diameter, and the tops were hinged so a person could access the inside as needed. The middle of the cage contained medium and small size eucalypt branches to allow the gliders outside perches. Two of the boxes had baby gliders who were now old enough to leave mama's pouch.

Nick carefully cupped his hands around a joey. Gently lifting it from the nest box, he handed it to Jen. The baby was half as big as the palm of Jen's hand and covered in beautiful soft fur. She held it briefly but was tenuous because it seemed fragile to her. When she handed it back to him, Nick put it away and pulled out an adult glider.

"This is the mama," he told her

Her body was as big as Jen's hand. The bushy tail was as long as it's body and covered in long, thick, soft fur. Like the flying squirrel, a membrane on each side of the body ran from the front to back legs allowing the animals the ability to glide. The fur on the back was blue-gray; it was cream colored on the belly. The cute animal had large dark eyes with three stripes on the head, its little round ears constantly twitched back and forth. Mama had a pouch on her lower belly in which she raised the babies until they were 70 days old.

Jen was thrilled. "What do they eat?"

"Wild gliders love the sweet sap from the eucalypts. They also eat pollen, and insects, mainly, moths and beetles, and even small vertebrates. I feed my gliders a diet used at the Taronga Zoo in Sydney. It includes apple, dog kibble, grapes, sweet potato, pear, banana, fly pupae, hard-boiled egg, papaya, honey, and high protein baby cereal.

"They're gorgeous and endearing!" Jen exclaimed. "Are they available in the states?"

"Not sure Luv. I think so. Follow me. I have some rare specimens to show you." He ushered the group out of the main cage and walked to a smaller one proudly showing the girls a group of color-mutated gliders. These were pure white gliders with dark eyes.

"Are these albinos?" Jen asked.

"Nope, these are true whites. See the black eyes? Albinos have no pigment whatsoever and have red eyes from the blood vessels in the back of the eye. I don't like the red eyes of the albinos. However, both albinos and white colored mutations are very scarce in captivity and command high prices if and when they're offered for sale."

Dr. Leighton's cell phone rang. She was needed on another farm to see a sick horse. Jen and Carrie thanked Nick for the tour as they left.

"Can we come with you?" Jen asked Doctor Leighton.

"No, it's too risky. I'll need to use my PPA suit. Best to take you back to the office first."

Chapter 14

Jocko

Rory was relaxing at home when the phone rang.

"Doc, it's Honey. Randy asked that I call about Jocko. He hasn't been acting right all evening."

"All day," Randy added in the background.

"Are you at the office, Honey? I hear someone with you."

"No, I'm staying at Jen's place while she's gone, to help Randy Remember I told you?"

"Oh, yeah. Okay, what's up?"

"Jocko got into Randy's broth bone leftovers yesterday. He vomited them up last night, and now he has blood in his vomit and stool," Honey added.

"You better bring him in. We have to run some tests and x-rays. I'll open the office up. Get there as soon as possible," Rory said. Sighing he hung up and put his shoes on.

Soon after arriving, Rory heard a vehicle coming up the drive. He opened the door ready to help carry Jocko inside.

"Where's Randy?" He asked when the driver door opened, and Honey came out. The light in the cab showed him Honey was alone.

"He'd rather you and I handle this by ourselves. I think Randy feels guilty. He hasn't called Jen yet."

"Do you need help bringing Jocko in, Honey?"

"No, he's moving around, just miserable, Doc," she replied as she opened the back door to let the award-winning Chesapeake out.

They brought Jocko directly to the treatment area.

"Help me lift him on the exam table," Rory said.

After helping Rory Honey walked to the treatment computer to set up the exam notes. "Ready," she said.

"Jocko presents alert and has a fever of 103.2. There is reddish-brown blood on the thermometer. Abdominal palpation is mildly painful in the upper belly, no abnormal or painful masses can be felt. He is stable, heart rate is 104, gums are pink, although cap refill is two seconds. He's going to need fluids," Rory added.

Blood was drawn for testing, and abdominal x-rays were done.

"See anything?" Honey asked Rory when he scanned the x-ray image.

"Nothing bad on the x-rays, but Jocko is dehydrated. Let's start an IV drip before lab results are finished. Can you shave his front leg? We need to put this catheter in," he said.

He jabbed the needle under Jocko's shaved skin, nodding is satisfaction when he saw blood filling the catheter.

He inserted a drip setup into the catheter and adjusted the flow.

"Keep the drips steady at three per second," he said. He heard the chemistry analyzer beep, walked to the machine and tore off the printed results.

"What does it say, Doc?" Honey asked.

"No abnormalities with liver, kidneys, electrolytes, although elevated proteins and globulins again suggest severe dehydration. And the test for pancreatitis flare-up is normal."

"What does it mean?"

"He's simply got an upset tummy. His over indulgence irritated the stomach and intestinal linings."

"Is he going to be okay?"

"Probably, Honey. We'll start him on Reglan to settle his stomach and add potassium because he was vomiting. But other than fluids he should be fine."

"Oh, good. Let me call Jen." Honey rummaged in her purse for her cellphone.

Rory was impressed. "You mean you can call Jen right now like she's across town?"

"Umm, hmm," Honey nodded, smiling. "She said something about buying a SIMs card. But the time is different. Australia is sixteen hours away. What time is it there?"

"It's 10:30 here, so Jen's seeing her clock say 4:30 pm."

"Good, I won't wake her up," Honey replied, as she put the phone to her ear.

"Hey Jen, it's Honey. I had to take Jocko to see Doc. He has a stomach ache."

She paused to listen.

"Everything's fine. Doc calls it garbage can enteritis. Here, Doc can explain it better, can't you?" She asked Rory.

He nodded. Smiling, he took the phone. "Hey Jen, how's your trip going?"

"Things are different here, Doc," Jen said. The men are assholes. What's going on with Jocko?"

"Just some indigestion from dietary indiscretion, Jen. I'm not worried. We gave Jocko an anti-vomit medicine as well as an anti-inflammatory to calm his inflamed stomach and intestines. Everything is stable, so I'm sending him home with Honey."

"So, I shouldn't be worried?"

"No, my worry level is below my knees."

"Is Randy there?"

"No, Honey brought him in. I guess Randy is worried you'd be angry at him."

Rory noticed Honey making signs she needed the phone back.

"Is there anything else?" Rory asked. "Honey wants to talk at you. Have a good time, Jen," he said as Honey grabbed the phone from him.

"Jen, can you do me a big favor?" Honey said excitedly. "You're in Queensland, right? Can you buy me a bottle of tea tree oil, please?"

"Tree-three oil? What's that, Honey" Jen asked.

"No, T-E-A, it is tea tree, it's an oil that comes from the melaleuca bush in Queensland," Honey replied. "It's used as an antifungal and antibacterial lotion."

"Sure."

"Thanks, Jen. Hey, tell me about your trip!" Honey said. "What is it like over there, in Australia in the middle of winter?"

"It's not the middle of winter, Honey. I am in the southern hemisphere and it is just past the summer solstice. But there is rainfall throughout the year, here, and everything is green. We go on horse and quad rides checking fence for damage from wild pigs. Billy carries two guns, a shotgun to kill snakes and birds, and a large caliber rifle that he uses to kill wild pigs whenever he finds them."

"Sounds like the wild west to me," Honey stated.

"Yeah, it is a bit that way," Jen said. "Billy has large ponds on the ranch which offer him access to waterfowl throughout the year, although his Queensland Heelers don't know anything about retrieving. That's why he wants a Chessie pup. His Heelers only know how to bark and to nip at the legs of cows that are being gathered up."

"I've always wanted a Queensland Heeler," Honey said. "When are you coming home?"

"Pounder will be released from quarantine next week. I have arranged to fly home from Sydney after I hand the pup over to Billy."

"So that's almost two more weeks. What are you doing with your spare time?"

"I'm repainting the inside of Billy's farmhouse and also spending time with Billy's sister, Carrie."

"That doesn't sound very interesting."

"No, it's good. Carrie has shown me around Brisbane, and she has taken me to visit a farmer who has an aviary full of furry little flying squirrels that are called sugar gliders. One can fit into the palm of my hand, and they are cute and like being petted.

"They sound adorable. You should bring one home!"

"We'll see."

"Well, Jen, I miss you, and can't wait for you to come home!"

"Soon," promised Jen, as she clicked her phone off.

Chapter 15

Gatton To Sydney

Over the next two weeks, Jen continued her painting and Billy grew to appreciate the bright white walls; he simply didn't show it. But his outbreaks were less frequent. Jen kept her opinion of the man to herself, but under her breath, she frequently called him a 'bogan.' It was her new favorite word, and it was more dismissive than arrogant. A Bogan brings problems wherever he goes because he doesn't know how to think.

Irrespective of the Bogan title, deserved or not, Billy was pleased. He hadn't felt this at home since Holly died. It was nice having a woman's touch again, but he would never admit it to Jen.

Billy tended the station daily. Mick helped when he was available. They all met up at supper in Nell and Ian's kitchen, and Jen began to feel she was a part of the family. At least now she had something to contribute.

Jen and Nell grew closer as they were near each other daily. Nell possessed the wisdom of age and was patient to explain. She was a teacher whom Jen sought out. Jen had never had a female figure in her life. She was at odds with her mother until her death a few years before. Saying goodbye to Nell was going to be difficult, as Jen had come to rely on her for moral and intellectual support. And she enjoyed her.

"Pounder is being released this Monday, Billy. I need to get to Sydney. I'll fly, I don't want to drive."

"No Jen you don't have to do that," Billy said. "I'll be happy to take you on a journey south. We'll take Hwy 1. There are spots along the way I want to show you."

Jen was taken back somewhat by such kindness from this gruff farmer, but it sounded like it would be fun in spite of him. "Sure, I'd love that Billy, thanks for offering."

Satisfied, he smiled proudly.

"Sorry, but I need to add one condition," Jen said.

"Go on," he nodded, willing to listen.

"I want to go to the Taronga Zoo to look at the sugar gliders."

"Not a problem!" Billy replied.

Two days before the quarantine was to be lifted Jen packed up her belongings and Billy helped her load them into his Land Rover. Jen had tears in her eyes as she hugged Nell goodbye promising to stay in touch.

Billy showed little emotion as he finished packing. After Jen offered tearful goodbyes they headed towards Brisbane. He drove south skirting the southern suburbs. At lunchtime, they stopped to eat at the Big Banana Café. It had a gigantic concrete banana in front, constructed years earlier as a way to induce tourists to stop in the middle of this subtropical territory. When Jen saw the banana, she laughed, "That is as gaudy as the giant wood Paul Bunyan statue we have on our Pacific Coast Highway in northern California."

After lunch, they continued south. Three hours later Billy pulled into the town of Forster. "I'm getting tired," he announced. "We need to stop for the day."

"I can drive," Jen offered.

"No. I'm the one escorting you and it's time to stop," Billy replied as he pulled into the parking area of a small motor lodge. "Wait here while I book us rooms." He went into the office and came out holding a key. "I've booked us a suite with an oceanfront view," he explained as he drove the car onto a small road to the ocean part of the lodge. "They only had one suite available, but it has two beds," he said. "I'll take the single bed, and you can have the double. Will that be okay with you?"

"It'll have to be," Jen replied. If she didn't know better, she would have thought this was a set-up, but she knew Billy wasn't like that. Besides she was a big girl and could handle the situation.

After entering the room, they realized it was a small apartment with a good-sized kitchenette, a stove, and all of the necessary utensils for cooking. And there were two bedrooms with a separate sitting room area.

"This looks great Billy! I thought we were going to be squeezed together in a small room. This will work out fine."

"Yep, it is quite nice, isn't it? We need to figure dinner. We could cook it ourselves if there is a grocery around here. Or would you prefer to eat at a diner?"

"Let's go out and see what we can find," Jen replied. "This is exciting, a whole new adventure."

Billy smiled at Jen's enthusiasm. He was enjoying her company, a feeling he thought he had lost completely. Not that Jen was anything like Holly, not at all. But she was a happy person and able to find joy in everything she did.

He had watched her while she worked her way through the house, cleaning and painting the walls. She even repainted the kitchen cupboards. It would have been a dull grueling chore for him, but Jen changed into her paint clothes every morning and sang and hummed her way through the day.

When she finished, Billy was amazed at how much better it looked. Jen refused to accept any compliments, insisting she was glad to help. It was an excellent gift for him, much better than the cakes and pies left by his admirers.

He also caught himself thinking of her at odd times: *I'll have to tell Jen about this,* or *Jen should be here to see this. Now, what is this all about? Jen is a married woman from halfway around the world. Oh well. No need to dwell. I'm hungry and need to find some grub.*

When Jen came out of the bathroom, Billy asked her: "How about we take a walk and see what food is out there?"

"That sounds great! Suddenly I'm starving."

The sound of the waves and the calling of the seagulls came to them when they left the suite, and a salty warm breeze played around them as they made their way through town. Forster was not very large; they ran out of town without finding any food store, so they settled on a restaurant. Hog's Breath was a steakhouse.

They hadn't spoken much during the drive that day. Jen tried to start a conversation a few times, but Billy was one of those drivers who focused primarily on the task at hand leaving little time for idle chitchat. It wasn't his forte anyway. Jen was glad she brought a book and spent her time reading, looking up when Billy pointed out different sights along the way.

Today was the first time they had been alone together since the horseback ride. Jen was comfortable with him while in the company of others. Now however, after the quiet ride, she was not sure how this evening with him was going to go. *We'll be like an old couple, running out of things to say to each other,* she thought.

The dinner was pleasant. It wasn't just the food which was good, but Billy and Jen actually conversed. Neither of them lost their temper, steering clear of any subject that could ignite an argument. Instead, they talked about themselves, sharing their childhoods, their homes, their dogs, and their memories.

When Billy asked Jen about Randy, she became quiet for a moment before she replied. "He's a good man Billy, but he has a hard time letting other people into his world. We make good partners as we mostly stay out of each other's way. I have always had hobbies that consume me, and he accepts that."

"Is that what you want out of marriage?" Billy asked.

"No, not really, but Randy is the only man I have been with who lets me be independent. I suspect he likes it because he can ignore me most of the time." She didn't know why but saying that made her cry.

Now Billy was flustered, uncomfortably so. "I'm sorry Jen. I didn't mean anything by it."

"Don't fret Billy it's me feeling sorry for myself. This is my second marriage to Randy He remarried after our divorce, and his third wife suffered a terrible accident at the Grand Canyon and died. I felt sorry for him and we started seeing each other again. I married him for the financial security more than anything else and I thought he was over Donna. But now he's running all over the west looking for her memories. I was hoping deep down he'd want to come with me on this trip."

"Here?"

"Yes, to Australia. I thought it might bring us closer. But now that I've been with you and Nell and Ian I have seen a way to rebuild my marriage."

"I see," he said. He didn't understand what she was talking about but nodded politely. "How?" he finally asked her.

"His family has a farm, and I intend to be more a part of it than I have been. The Bianchis are an exclusive club, and I haven't tried very hard to break into it. It will be difficult, but I think it will make both of us happier. Then, hopefully, everything will fall into place."

"What if it doesn't?"

"Then I'm ready to move on. This time I'll look for a relationship that is more loving. Do you know what I mean?"

"Certainly, but a good partnership is a significant part of it, don't you think?"

"Oh yes, it is! That's what has kept us together. We understand each other that way. However, there's no spark. Oh shit. I sound like one of those whiny housewives who have affairs because they are never satisfied. I'm not... fulfilled and I am doing Randy a disservice. I love him, I need him, and I want him, but I feel it is one sided. I didn't intend to dump on you like this, I'm sorry."

"Holly and I weren't together long enough in our marriage to reach that point. But I also have these images of marriage that I will never be able to recreate you know?"

"Yeah, it would be a hard spell to break."

They were both lost in their thoughts when she said: "Can I ask you a very personal question?"

"I suppose," Billy replied nervously not sure if he wanted to answer.

"Have you had another woman since Holly?"

No answer. Billy took a big gulp of wine and Jen did the same. He hadn't spoken about Holly to any other woman before.

"I owe you an honest answer; you have been forthright with me. The answer is no, for a lot of reasons. At first, it was pure sorrow. We loved each other so much, and we were such good friends, and Holly was so unique. I, all of us, missed her for a long time, maybe too long. By the time the pain ebbed years had passed. When I finally did pick my head up and look around everyone in the area seemed too close. They all knew Holly, and I felt her memory would get in the way of a new relationship."

Jen was moved by Billy's openness. She saw a side of him she would never have seen if they had not found a chance to talk away from the influence of the station and his family. She stifled the urge to touch him, to hold and comfort him. *It would not be right, would it?* They had been together for almost four weeks, but they didn't know each other. Up until now, they shared little, other than courtesy with each other, and even that was circumspect. And now, well…

"Billy, I don't know why I asked you that. There's nothing I can do other than listen. I truly am sorry for your loss and I know how profound a loss it was for you. Do you feel the need for companionship? You could probably go online, possibly meet someone from another area who is not quite so close to your memories."

"Frankly, I haven't even felt that need until you showed up. I don't know, maybe having you in such close quarters is nudging me from my safe cocoon. I'm not used to this."

"Oh, Billy! I didn't mean to pry or upset you. I hope I haven't offended you." Jen reached over and put her hand on his. It felt warm and was very calloused, a workingman's hand. He didn't pull away but placed his other hand over hers and held it.

Their eyes met, and neither moved nor said a word. Jen's heart fluttered. *What is going on here?* She thought to herself.

Suddenly the waiter appeared "Will there be anything else? Possibly dessert?" That broke the spell. They both pulled away as if they had touched something hot.

"Do you want dessert?" Billy asked.

"No thanks, I'm good," Jen replied.

The walk back to the lodge was quiet, calming, and not uncomfortable. Jen slipped her hand in Billy's as they strolled down the hill. Pausing outside the door she gave him a brief friendly hug and they went inside.

"How long is it to Sydney, Billy?"

"A little over three hours, why do you ask?"

"Because I have a surprise for you! I booked us an exclusive tour of Australian native wildlife at the Taronga Zoo. The tour starts at 10:00 so we need to be gone from here before 6:00."

Billy laughed. "I already know Australian wildlife. I think this tour is more for you Jen. I reckon you wanted to see more sugar gliders."

Offended, Jen became quiet. Billy noticed and backtracked. "I'm sorry. I didn't mean to be rude. I would love to go. Right now, I'm drained, and I need to get to bed soon. I'll see you in the morning."

With that, he went into his room and closed the door.

The next day they had a quick breakfast of coffee and scones and headed straight toward Sydney driving into the Taronga Zoo parking lot. Jen went up to the gatehouse to find out where the adventure tour began and was told to go through the gate on the far left.

"Hurry!" she urged Billy as she grabbed his hand and pulled him along, deciding to keep him busy walking to minimize the complaining he was prone to.

A zookeeper called the group waiting for the tour and introduced himself.

"G'day! My name is Mitch and I am here to show you parts of the zoo generally off limits to most people."

The tour lasted an hour and a half. Mitch escorted the group through the zoo kitchen where people were chopping large amounts of fruits and vegetables. The venue was, as Jen expected, to provide up close experiences with koala bears, emus, wombats, echidnas, and bilbies as well as the duck-billed platypus one of the weirdest creatures she ever saw.

She hand-fed the kangaroos and wallabies and made sure Billy took a picture of her in the koala bear exhibit. Most importantly she was once again given a favorable experience with the sugar gliders. Mitch showed Jen a three-month-old joey that was venturing outside of mama's pouch, explaining how to open the pouch to see another joey firmly attached to a nipple. Jen decided there and then she wanted gliders of her own.

Chapter 16

Release from Quarantine

Jen needed to be in the western suburbs of Sydney between 1:30 and 3:30 to collect Pounder. Billy brought one of his dog carriers at Jen's request. He had three he used to transport his Heelers to other farms and stations to help round up the livestock. It was big enough to house Pounder comfortably.

"That looks like a bank deposit box with air vents in it," Jen observed.

"I had these custom-made. They are stainless steel and I think they'll last longer than I will."

Billy pulled up to the quarantine station, and Jen went inside to arrange the release. Billy went to the back of the Land Rover to retrieve the carrier. As he was wrangling the massive thing out of the vehicle, Jen appeared with a light-brown colored dog, wildly jumping and spinning around her at the end of his leash.

"Come over here, Billy!" Jen exclaimed. "Meet your new best friend!"

The dog's excitement diminished somewhat, when Billy approached them. Jen bent down to reassure her pup, patting him on his head as she introduced him to Billy.

"And this is going to be one of your new housemates, Pounder!" The happy dog wagged his tail vigorously when Billy petted him.

"Let's take him for a walk," Jen said. Billy pushed the kennel back into the car, locked it up, and they wandered the grassy roadway.

"Where are you staying tonight Billy?"

"I've arranged to go back to the place we stayed in Forster. The couple that runs the motel told me it would be okay to bring the dog inside if he stays in his kennel. When is your flight back home?"

"Not until tomorrow at one," Jen replied. She felt a sharp pang when she answered him. It was going to be hard for her to leave this place. She was very attached to Pounder and had grown close to Billy's family. Her mind raced for reasons to stay while her loyalties dictated she go home. Suddenly she blurted out. "I think I should stay here another two weeks or so. I haven't been with Pounder for over three weeks and I want to be sure he remembers his previous training. It will also make his transition here a good one. Yes, I need to stay here for a while longer," Jen convinced herself.

Billy showed surprise and concern although inwardly he was pleased with the change of plans. "Okay, then. Let's start our trip back."

"I have to call home first," Jen told him. "I'll meet you back at the car. Here you take Pounder."

Jen dialed home. It was near nine in the evening there, and Randy answered. "Hi sweetie, this is Jen checking in."

"Hi honey," Randy replied." Isn't it time for your flight home soon?"

"Well, that's why I'm calling. After being in the quarantine station for four weeks, I'm worried Pounder will feel lost without me…"

"Oh, for Christ's sake Jen! It makes no difference to Pounder if you leave now or in two years. You're going to have to let him go you know."

"I want to stay another two weeks. I can change my ticket and fly out of Brisbane."

"Whatever you want dear," Randy said impatiently. "I need you to remember you live here and not in Australia."

"I know baby, but things aren't right for me to leave now. How did the hand surgery go?"

"So-so. I may need more surgery depending on what the x-rays show in two weeks."

"Did they have to bandage your hand Randy?"

"Oh yeah. They bandaged me past my elbow."

"You sound relaxed; I'm happy to hear it. I want to sit down with you to make some plans. I've picked up some good ideas here."

"Like what?" Randy didn't like things to be sprung on him.

"Nothing groundbreaking, honey. I think we need to do more together, you and me."

"Okay. Call me when you plan to come home."

Jen walked back to the car. She needed to sort some feelings out to understand what drew her so strongly to this place and this family. Maybe it was the love and acceptance everyone showed. Deeper yet there was a caring the family members had for one another. Her marriage with Randy was stable but was missing something that she now knew she needed.

After the three-hour drive back, they stopped in Newcastle for a nice dinner because there were few culinary offerings available in Forster. Then Billy checked into the same suite they rented the night before.

Jen let Pounder out of his kennel and started down the street towards the beach to let him run. *He must have a lot of excess energy after spending a month in a cage with limited walks*, she thought.

Billy saw her walk away and ran to catch up with her. "Jen hang on. Wait for me."

As he reached her, he grabbed her hand, and they went on together. Once at the beach Jen let Pounder off leash. He took off for the water running and jumping at the blowing sand.

"He needs this," Jen said. "I don't think he's had a good run the whole time he's been in Australia. This is good for his body and his mind."

Standing there, watching Pounder, Jen realized she was still holding Billy's hand.

"Billy, I want you to understand why I stayed longer. It wasn't only for Pounder."

"I was hoping that wasn't the only reason. I may be wrong here, but I don't think I'm the only one who feels there is something between us, and it is not only friendship," Billy replied.

"Oh, Billy. I'm a married woman. I have no right to feel this way about you, but I can't help it."

"And I haven't felt like this since Holly died. Let's take Pounder back and get a bottle of wine. Maybe we can sort this out."

Jen collected the puppy, and they walked back to the lodge arm in arm.

It was a quiet, warm evening, so they kept the windows of their suite open. Sitting at the table sipping wine, they conversed quietly for several hours. As night fell and the sky darkened they didn't bother to turn on the lights. The darkness enhanced the intimacy of their conversation.

Jen realized she was growing very fond of this man. He was a wounded soul, but he was strong and brave, managing to keep himself together and raise his son in spite of his tremendous loss. She could not believe he had spent so many years alone yet now he was willing to open up to her. She felt an awesome responsibility not to hurt him, but she was also thrilled at the same time.

They moved to the sofa in the small sitting room. For a while they were silent, holding hands.

"You are so soft," Billy whispered. "I've forgotten how soft women are."

Feeling a rush of emotions, she reached up to touch his face. He leaned down and kissed her as tears fell down her cheeks.

"I don't want to hurt you Billy, and I don't want to hurt Randy either."

"We don't have to do this Jen. We can stop here."

"I can't stop here. I want you. I want to feel you inside me. I want all of you."

Billy stood up and gently took her hand. She followed him into his bedroom.

Their lovemaking consumed them. Billy was a quiet lover attentive to her needs, and Jen gave all of herself to him. It seemed so natural for them to be lovers, so right somehow. And for a while, she forgot Randy and her life back in California. She was oblivious to anything outside of this moment in this small room with this incredibly loving man.

As the sky lightened with the dawn, they fell into an exhausted sleep embracing one another.

After breakfast, they headed home. Billy had no cell phone because he never needed one. Now he asked Jen if she could call ahead to Nell to let her know what the schedule was. Jen called the number.

"Nell this is Jen. Pounder seems to have lost his training during the quarantine stay. I felt it would be better if I came back with him to make sure he evens out."

"Wonderful!" Nell exclaimed. "I'll have dinner ready for everyone!"

When they drove into the station, Jen felt guilty. Nell prepared a homecoming party. Mick and Carrie both came in from town. The table setting was lavish.

"Hello there, Jen. It is good to see you again." Carrie hugged her hard, giggling harder. She snuggled close to Jen's ear and whispered: "This is such a treat. We're going to have such a good time."

"What are you talking about Carrie?"

"You and Billy slept together."

"What makes you think that? Stop it, Shh."

Billy gave Mick his new present. Pounder readily accepted Mick as the young man grabbed the dog's ears, shook his head back and forth, and thumped him playfully on his back.

"Jen has agreed to stay and help train this dog for a few more days," Billy said.

"Good for you Pops!" Nick congratulated his Dad.

After dinner, they sat out on the veranda drinking beer and wine. Jen told Carrie of the visit to the Taronga Zoo, especially about the sugar gliders.

"I'm falling in love with these creatures," she confided to Carrie. "Can you arrange another trip out to the glider farm?"

"No problem," Carrie replied as she took out her phone and began checking her diary.

The next day Jen and Carrie took Pounder out to one of the lakes. Jen wanted to evaluate his retrieving abilities. The girls put half a dozen duck decoys into the back of the quad and drove out to a large lake with a jetty and a rowboat. Mick and Billy followed after them in another four-wheel-drive, with shotguns. The men stayed on the shore while the women and Pounder jumped into the boat and rowed it toward the center of the lake.

Jen stood up and threw the decoys into the water. They wanted the real ducks to think this was a safe place to land. But Pounder jumped out of the boat and immediately swam out to each decoy bringing each safely back to the craft one at a time. Everybody bent over laughing. Here was a top of the line retriever who didn't know the difference between real and fake ducks.

Jen was embarrassed but suggested Pounder was still too young to understand all the nuances of his duties. Billy agreed that Pounder was not ready for such high-intensity training. He was excited to know that the dog retrieved instinctively. He would wait a month then work with a mate he knew.

Jen knew she had chosen well for her dog, feeling he would grow to be a well-disciplined happy fellow. She found herself watching Billy several times that day and he seemed to be very near her whenever possible.

During the ride back to the house Carrie and Jen got separated from the men. They were excitedly chattering when Carrie blurted out: "Okay, what's going on with you and Billy? You two did sleep together, didn't you?"

Jen was silent for a moment. *Should I tell her? Will Carrie hate me for what I've done?* This was important to Jen. She didn't want to lose this friendship she had so much come to love. Carrie was such a straightforward person Jen would be truthful with her no matter the outcome. And it surprised her, this sudden gushing forth of emotions.

"Billy and I made love last night Carrie," she confessed.

Carrie stomped the brakes, sliding to an immediate stop, and almost tossing Pounder out of the quad.

"I knew it!" Carrie shouted as she started laughing. She wrapped her arms around Jen and hugged her hard. "You don't know how happy that makes me! Billy has needed this for so long and I'm so glad it was you!"

"Carrie?" Jen was overwhelmed. She had not expected this response. She felt so accepted, so loved, and so grateful that Carrie understood. "I don't know why it happened, but it did."

"I had a feeling you did. You both seem happier and are more relaxed around each other. Oh, this is beautiful!"

"So, you don't need an explanation?"

"Oh, it doesn't matter why. You can't predict what your heart will want. It's such a beautiful thing when you find love. It is love, isn't it?"

"It sure feels like love Carrie. I'm bewildered right now, but I do love him. He is a generous, loving man. How could I not feel that way?"

"Billy hasn't shown that side of himself to anyone but family for so long. Whatever happens from this, he will be a better man for it. He can be whole again."

Jen started to cry. "Oh, Carrie. I hope I haven't hurt him. I feel so selfish right now."

Carrie grabbed Jen's hand. "I don't know where you are with your husband Jen, but I do know I haven't seen Billy smile like he did today in a long, long time. He's a big boy; he can handle whatever you decide. You simply opened up a tightly closed door for him sweetie. Don't worry on Billy's account."

"You think he'll be okay?"

"Yes, I think he will. We better not tell Mum or Mick of this though. We don't want to get too many people involved because it could mess things up."

"I don't know what's going to happen with this. Billy and I have agreed not to do it again. I have so much to think on, and he does too. I need to straighten things out at home; I owe Randy that. I owe Billy that. Heck, I owe myself that."

"Tell me your history. When did you get married to Randy? Wasn't that a long time ago?"

"This is our second marriage to each other. I married him first when Nancy, his first wife, died. Then we married again after Donna, his third wife, died in the Grand Canyon."

"Really? How did these ladies die, Jen?" Carrie looked at her open-mouthed. "I'd be nervous as hell to be alone with this fellow."

"Well I didn't die, I divorced his ass. And those deaths were accidents, Carrie."

"Umm," Carrie was shaking her head. "One maybe, but two? I don't know Jen. How many men do you know who have two dead wives? This doesn't make sense to me. I thought you were smarter than that."

"Wow! Don't be afraid to tell me how you feel, Carrie. Not that it's your business, but I'm not trying to hide anything. There are a lot of things I still love about Randy, and the things I don't like, I can ignore. I love living on the ranch, and I love my friends there. So, Randy and I made a deal. He wanted to be married again and I told him I'd come back if he let me breed Chesapeake Bay Retrievers."

Carrie started up the quad shaking her head. "Well, I don't understand any of this." The girls didn't talk the rest of the way home, but Carrie had a smile on her face the whole time.

That night as Jen soaked in the tub she forged a plan. She was drawn to this family and especially to Billy, but she had a life back home, and she had a husband she needed to go back to. Randy didn't deserve this. He would be blindsided by it.

"Oh Randy, what have I done to you?" she sighed.

She would have to put this thing with Billy away somewhere. She couldn't tell her husband; it would be too hurtful.

It was only a one-time thing, she told herself.

She would go home with a new resolve to make her marriage work. She could make it work. There was no other choice. She would make this work.

I can create this feeling of family with Randy, she thought. *Yes, I can make this happen.* That night Jen slept a deep and dreamless sleep.

The next morning Carrie popped into the room and sat on Jen's bed. "Hey, sleepy head! It's time to do something adventuresome. Let's go back to the sugar glider farm."

"Alright," Jen replied groggily. "Does Nell have coffee made yet?"

"Yep. Here, put some clothes on. We are on a mission!"

"Wait, I need to let Pounder out of his kennel and take him on his morning walk," Jen said as she jumped out of bed.

"Okay, I'll be over with Mum."

Jen leashed Pounder, took him for his morning walk, and worked some obedience maneuvers with him. After they had coffee she and Carrie drove off to Nick O'Reilly's station to give Jen more experience with gliders.

The white gliders fascinated her. Although illegal in California she could purchase regular colored gliders in Nevada. But she wanted this strain because their black eyes contrasted so beautifully with the soft white fur.

Nick explained more on the genetics of the color. "Most of the time this white color is a recessive genetic trait, which means that breeding this color is a crapshoot. However, I've performed extensive line breeding on my two first adults and have diluted the normal colored genes down enough to create more whites than normals."

"Wow! Now I have got to have these fellows," Jen said.

"Oh, you mean to take some back to the states with you? Ya can't. It is a bit illegal to remove gliders from Oz," Nick replied.

"A bit illegal is incorrect. It is downright criminal!" Carrie said.

Jen started to argue. "But this strain is no longer native anyway. You would be doing a disservice to the environment if they ever escaped."

"Point taken," Nick conceded. "Well, it's your neck, not mine. I have a feeling if I don't sell them to you, you'll get them somewhere else. So, let's do this."

The girls thanked the man and jumped into Carrie's car. Jen couldn't stop talking about the white gliders, but Carrie had had enough. "Oh, for Christ's sake leave it alone!" she said. "We have much better things to talk about." She winked at Jen as if they were conspirators and Jen laughed. She loved this redheaded girl.

Carrie stayed for dinner that evening, but Mick was back in Gatton. "So, how's the new pup working out?" Billy asked Jen.

"He's adjusting well," Jen replied. "He's quiet and has no worries sleeping in his new kennel."

"Why is he in a kennel?" Billy asked.

"So, he can be close to me as he gets used to his new place."

"Close to you? Where did you keep him last night?"

"His kennel is in my bedroom, Billy."

"I do not want dogs inside the house," Billy exclaimed as he pounded his fist on the table. The old Billy suddenly emerged with a vengeance.

"Goddammit Billy! Didn't you listen to anything I told you when we were setting this up! I said over and over again how much this breed needs human interaction!" Jen angrily pushed her chair from the table and stormed out of the house. Maybe; it wouldn't be so hard to stay away from Billy after all.

Chapter 17

Sugar Gliders

Jen was irritated. Billy listened only to what he wanted to hear. She pulled out a bottle of wine from the kitchen in the little house and drew up a bathtub full of steamy water. Slipping into the tub, she arranged her wine glass and bottle to be near. Her irritation would subside and then flare up again, and again, until the warm water, and the chardonnay soothed her down.

Jen was concerned that Pounder would not get the attention he deserved once she left. Every one of her Chessies were hand-reared in a human environment to bring out the strongest loyalty from each dog. Now this training might be undone because the stubbornness of a man from Oz dictated he follow the same precise bullshit every other Australian had been doing for the past one hundred fifty years. There would be no problem for her to return home with Pounder; no quarantine was required upon entry into California.

As she sipped her wine Jen's mind became more creative.

If I bring Pounder back home in one of those homemade stainless-steel kennels, OMG, I could also arrange to have a hidden box fabricated to store sugar gliders! The box could be made to look like it was a shelf under the vent holes at the top, she reasoned. *The breeder said sugar gliders don't need a whole lot of space and feel more comfortable when tightly confined.* She decided she would discuss this with Nell.

Billy was checking fence line the next morning when Jen went over for coffee. Nell was surprised the two had reached such an impasse on Pounder and immediately took Jen's side.

"I'll take Pounder," Nell offered. "I've always wanted a house dog and Billy can elect not to come to my house if he is so offended by this idea. I'll talk to him and tell him I want Pounder to stay here with me, and you're welcome to move into the big house too."

"Okay, we'll move Pounder over to your place straight away," Jen decided. "Come on over, and I'll introduce you to each other."

Jen went back to the small house she had called home for the last four weeks, noticing it was much brighter now, thanks to her painting. A twinge of disappointment settled over her.

Oh well, this is for the best, she thought. She and Billy needed some separation if they were going to keep to their promise. With Carrie knowing of their tryst, it didn't seem like such a secret. But still, Jen felt they needed to keep it from everyone else. She wondered if Carrie had talked to Billy about the affair or if she intended to do so in the future. *Would Billy be angry if Carrie broached the subject?* He seemed to be back to his old nasty self again. *What a grump!*

Jen finished packing the last of her clothes when she heard the backdoor slam. *Here we go,* she thought apprehensively. "Billy is that you?"

"Who else would it be? Of course, it's me."

This was going to be hard anyway, and she hoped he would have used up some of his anger, fixing fence. Obviously not.

She walked out of the bedroom carrying her bags and set them down by the front door. Billy sat at the kitchen table and looked up at her.

"What are you doing?" he asked acrimoniously.

Jen paused for a moment and then said in a rush: "Pounder and I are moving over to the big house for the rest of my stay. It's not because of you Billy, although you do seem to have reverted to your old habits again. It's for Pounder."

Jen babbled on giving Billy no time to respond. "I know you don't agree. You've made that very plain. But I know my dogs, and this is a crucial time for this puppy. He needs a person to bond with to allow him to feel he is part of this family and not some outside doormat. Nell has offered to take him and I'm going to move over there as well. She tells me she has always wanted an inside dog, but you men have always been against it. I know it's necessary for Pounder and I also believe it's the best for you and me."

She stopped out of breath and waited for him to speak. While she was giving her speech, she saw the emotions passing over his face like storm clouds. Now he simply sat.

There was a long silence. *Should I go?* She thought. As she turned away, he cleared his throat, and she turned back.

He was crying.

"Oh, Billy I'm not leaving yet."

"I know. But this kind of ends it, doesn't it?" He replied softly.

"Well, that was what we agreed to you know. It's not easy for me either, believe me."

"I'm sorry I have been so coarse with you lately. I'm trying to adjust to your departure. You have grown on me Sheila, and I don't want to see you go."

"I'll still be here for twelve more days Billy. Please let's make the best of it. I love you. I don't know if you know that, but it will never change. I only want you to be happy."

"I'm happy whenever I see or think about you Jen. And, I know I'll learn to be happy without you. It'll take time. Here let me help you with your move. I'm sure Mum will be glad for the company."

By dinner that night Billy was almost cheerful again. Well, it was cheerful for Billy's standards. Nell seemed pleased they had gotten over another hurdle. Jen began Pounder's house training by teaching him to lie quietly and not beg at the table.

Now that Pounder was staying she would have to find another dog to bring home. She needed a secret place for her gliders. The next day she approached Billy with her problem. "Billy, I need your help and advice on something.

"Aye, what's on your mind, Jen?"

"Can you arrange for the construction of one of your stainless-steel dog kennels for me?"

"I don't see why not."

"Good. I also want to purchase a young Queensland Heeler pup for a friend of mine back home."

"No problem."

Jen paused, ready to drop the sugar glider bombshell on the fellow. "And one more thing, I need your help for a little subterfuge I am planning."

"Wait, what are you talking about?" Billy became concerned.

"I have been talking with Nick O'Reilly, and we agreed on a price for two pairs of white sugar gliders. I plan on bringing them back to California."

"You might find yourself in a lot of trouble if you get caught. Those animals are restricted!"

"I know, but by hiding them inside a box in the kennel, I will be able to bring them into the U.S. undetected. Dogs from Australia don't have to be quarantined to enter the states. They can be picked up in the terminal upon arrival. The small box the sugar gliders are in is going to look like a shelf underneath the vents at the top of the kennel. These are the white gliders. They are not the gliders the Aussie officials are trying to protect. And if these white ones ever escaped they could easily be seen by predators and picked off for food.

"I'll help arrange this for you, Jen, but you need to know that you'll be on your own if you get caught."

"I'm used to being on my own anyway Billy."

Jen borrowed Billy's Rover to drive to Nick's station to make sure everything was in line. Billy talked with Nick to make sure the stainless-steel cage would work as needed. Nick altered the design, placing the secret box along the back of the crate to allow the cloth nesting pouches a vertical hang that mimicked their regular environment. He added long slits on the sides of the box to allow adequate air transfer. Then Billy took Jen to a Queensland Heeler breeder to arrange the purchase of a puppy.

Jen arranged for her departure from Brisbane and called home. She left a message for Randy to come up to SFO to get her and her cargo from the international terminal.

As departure day neared and the frantic last-minute details finalized Jen had time to reflect on her choices. She was

91

determined to throw herself into her marriage. She had taken it too lightly for too long. Hopefully, she would find at least some of what Billy and Holly knew. It was possible; by prioritizing her relationship with Randy, she felt she could achieve this goal at least to some extent.

The departure date arrived. Jen hugged Nell goodbye and tried to enter the wrong side of the land rover as she wiped away tears. Billy walked from the house, spoke a bit to Nell, got in the truck and drove Jen to the Brisbane Airport.

Jen began sobbing. "I'm sorry Billy. I'm trying to do the right thing. I'm trying to save my marriage."

Billy didn't reply. He nodded, patted Jen's leg, and continued staring straight ahead.

Chapter 18

Back to San Francisco

Fourteen hours after leaving Brisbane, the plane was in a circling pattern around the San Francisco Bay Peninsula waiting for its turn to land. "Ladies and gentlemen, we are on a landing approach into San Francisco. Please return your tables and seats to their upright positions, turn off all electrical devices and fasten your seatbelts. We will be landing in a few minutes."

Once it touched down the plane taxied to the international terminal. Because this flight was coming from outside the US the passengers and their belongings were searched by US Customs to make sure that all entries were legal. While Jen was having her bags searched she wondered how the animals in the kennel were getting on.

"Excuse me ma'am, but what is this?" the customs officer asked Jen.

"Oh, that's called tea tree oil. I picked it up for a friend of mine. It is a mixture of herbs from one of those trees back in Australia. The melaleuca tree, I think."

"Well, it doesn't have any export labels on it. I am going to have to confiscate it."

"Fine, do what you need to do," Jen replied irritated. Soon afterward the suitcases were closed, and Jen was allowed to walk into United States territory legally. As she made her way to the main terminal she found Randy searching for her.

"Hi Randy!" she said. "Boy, have I missed you."

"Me too," Randy replied, as the two embraced for a long time.

Jen started to cry.

"What's wrong, dear?"

"Nothing serious. It's just been so long, and so many different things have happened to me in the last six weeks. I'm relieved to be back home."

Randy was confused. Jen rarely showed outward emotions. It made him uneasy with the situation; he didn't know how to respond. "Here, let me help you with your luggage. I want to take you out for a bite to eat before we drive back home."

"We can't do that. I have to pick up a kennel from customs animal area."

"What!? You brought Pounder back?"

"No, I brought home a Queensland Heeler for Honey."

"Oh."

"And there is another surprise inside the kennel."

Randy exhaled. *Here comes more of Jen's animal stuff,* he thought to himself. He sighed. "Now what have you brought home?"

"Little furry, fuzzy, cute, bat type creatures called sugar gliders. You need to wait here. You don't have an international ticket, so you can't follow me back to the animal area. I'll be back within a half hour. Why don't you take the luggage to the truck, and wait at the curb?"

Randy mumbled something and dutifully followed Jen's directions. Jen went to the animal area, showed her ID and her ticket, and collected the kennel. She found a cart and headed out to the curb. Randy saw Jen, jumped out of the truck and helped her load the kennel into the back seat.

"I have to find a store, a grocery that sells greens. The sugar gliders haven't eaten for almost twenty-four hours."

"It's not easy to find a food store in San Bruno, Jen. It's either freeway or hotel."

"Try to go into the center… oh, I don't know either, Randy" She looked at him. "Thanks for putting up with me and my moods all these years Randy"

"You're welcome."

"Oh, stop!" Jen said suddenly. "Here's a store. Pull in here; I'll be right back."

Jen bought apples, dog kibble, grapes, bananas, papaya, and honey. She pulled down the tailgate of the truck and began peeling and chopping and mixing everything together. "Viola! Instant sugar glider diet, inspired by the folks from down under. I also bought a bottle of wine, we can open it a few minutes before getting home."

"Another Australian inspiration, no doubt." He bantered.

"Maybe so, but at least I didn't bring home a jar of Vegemite. It's this gooey, kind of spread that smells like cod liver oil. They carry on about it; they all need their daily fix," she giggled. "Can you walk this dog please Randy, while I feed these little guys? It would really help."

Realizing the quicker she was finished the sooner they would get home, he was eager to help as much as possible. Jen let the puppy out of its kennel; he took the leash and turned.

"Randy, come here," Jen said as he started to walk away with the bouncing, happy puppy. She kissed his cheek. "Thank you, Baby." He nodded his head with a satisfied smile and headed for a nearby patch of grass. Jen opened the secret box to give the gliders more room and fed them the nourishment they desperately needed. When she was sure they were full, she tucked them all back into their cozy roost and waited for Randy to return. With the dog was back in its kennel, they started out again. Jen chatted on for most of the drive home telling him about her experiences and how different Australia and Australians were. As they turned into the drive to their ranch house, she was describing the aviary Nick built. "Can you do that for me, Randy?" she asked.

"No problem, dear."

"Oh, and one more thing."

"Yes, Dear."

"They had this big old bathtub that I sat in almost every night. I really want a tub like that." Randy jumped on the idea.

"That sounds great! We can get one of those spa tubs and put it in the guest bathroom."

Jen smiled. *Maybe this marriage has some hope, after all,* she thought.

Chapter 19

Honey and King

"So, this is a real Queensland Heeler from Queensland Australia!" Rory exclaimed to Jen squatting down to pet the dog up close. "Hey there, how do you like America? I'm impressed, he looks good. Now let's put him through an exam." He lifted the mellow puppy from the scale to the exam table.

Rory liked the healthy feel of his coat, the amount of muscle on the young dog, and his demeanor in general. Placing his stethoscope to his ears, he continued his evaluation.

"Heart and lungs are fine. Heart rate is 120; Temp is 102.8." He reported to Honey as she typed the findings into the computer. He hesitated a moment. "His temp is slightly elevated. I wasn't expecting much over 102 more like 101.5. Was he okay at the inspection in Australia Jen?"

"As near as I can tell, yeah, he was passed by a vet too. Why are you asking?"

"It's his high temp."

Draping the stethoscope around his neck, he rubbed both of the puppy's ears. Moving to the front, he looked into the dog's eyes.

"Ears are fine, eyes WNL, no nasal discharge."

Smiling he placed both hands on the dog's head gently prying the mouth open. "Teeth look good, no tarter and the bite is fine."

The testicles were descending as expected, and he found no painful spots when he manipulated the shoulders, elbows, hips, and stifle joints. "This dog looks in good shape, but we need to watch the temp. It should come down as he gets acclimated Jen."

"That's up to Honey," Jen said. "I'm giving the dog to her."

Rory looked at Honey who was smiling and nodding.

"This is a present from me to Honey." Jen said. "From Australia. Sorry about the Tea Tree Oil, they're so strict about some things it's unbelievable. Good thing I didn't tell him I bought a bra there."

"Really, are you sure, Jen?" Honey asked one final time.

"He's yours Honey," Jen smiled.

"That's so cool, thanks Jen."

"What are you naming him?"

"His name is Southern King or King for short," she said, proudly.

"Well good. Hey King, how's it going?" Rory fluffed and pounded the puppy playfully.

"I would like to bring him to work with me, is that okay Doc?"

"Yep, so long as he isn't a nuisance."

Chapter 20

Sugar Glider Babies

Jen was outside with her dogs when Sandra, her neighbor arrived to discuss horses.

"You've got to see my sugar gliders," Jen said.

"What are sugar gliders?"

"Come behind the barn, and I'll show you."

Jen showed her to an outside walk-in birdcage Randy adapted for sugar gliders.

"This cage is nice, Jen" Sandra said.

"It's called an aviary, and it's usually for birds, but it can hold these guys easily," Jen answered. "Randy made it for me. The foundation was here from a previous shed or something, so it was easy to put up the cage sides and tin roof."

"That's neat," Sandra said. "Can he make one for me? I want some gliders too. But Byron isn't motivated to use any tools other than a gun and a fishing pole."

"I'll ask. Follow me. The sugar gliders love it here," Jen added proudly.

"How can you tell?" Sandra asked as they walked into the aviary, speaking in a softer tone for they were inside the gliders' realm.

"By being observant and paying attention to them. But, those are things you already do."

"Why do you say that?"

"Because you're so good with training birds and animals, which is what this takes." Jen paused as she counted the gliders. It was an automatic inventory she did every time she entered their enclosure. There were still four of them.

"How many do you have?"

"I have two pairs. Once they have babies, I will have anywhere from four to six, maybe seven."

"Do they have a breeding season?"

"In Australia, they breed year-round. But I may have screwed that up moving them here."

"Why?"

"Their seasons flipped when I brought them north of the equator."

"How much money can you make from them, do you think?"

"Five thousand apiece, male or female. As long as they're white."

"I'm interested Jen," Sandra said. "Selling babies can pay for feed and cages, my most expensive items. When are you selling yours?"

"I'm not sure. If I breed these six for ten or fifteen generations, I should have dozens of high-priced gliders. Let's see how easy it is to raise a litter or gaggle or whatever they call them."

"Well, keep the door open for me girlfriend," Sandra said smiling.

"You bet," Jen replied while gently searching the nest box.

"What do you mean they may have a breeding problem?" Sandra asked.

"I moved them from the southern hemisphere. Their biological clocks have to switch to a reverse season. I didn't expect babies for four or more months. I'm ready to wait a year, but...."

"But what?"

"I think we have babies," Jen said in a confidential tone. "I saw moving bumps in the pouches of both of my females."

"Can I touch one?" Sandra asked.

"You can try, but they're still kind of jumpy. Here let's take a look at Sophie, she's the tamest. Hey there," Jen said softly.

Sophie replied with a clicking chucking noise as Jen offered her a treat. Jen gently caressed her belly and she chortled in protest. Then she bit her and scampered into the recesses of her nest box.

"The baby joeys are born after sixteen days when they are the size of a jelly bean," Jen continued. "They squirm out and find their way to a nipple inside mother's pouch. It's usually a few weeks after birth when we notice the mothers' pouches look extended."

"When do they come outside of the pouch?"

"After two months, they begin jumping in and out until mama boots them out for good, around two months later."

"When can she become pregnant again?"

"Anytime. Once she kicks the joeys out and gives her pouch and nipples a quick break her heat cycles return."

***

These furry marsupials were easy to raise, given Jen's instinctive feel for what animals need to keep them happy. She was like a fertilizer is for a vegetable garden. By September the joeys were forced to declare their independence and began foraging totally on their own. Jen was handling them when Janie came over with Sandra.

"How are the babies? Janie asked.

"There were four joeys. Only two of them were the white color we want…"

"Oh, that drops our projections in half," Sandra demurred.

"I know," Jen was sad too. "But they are really cool. If all four live I'll sell you one of each, because I need your help to make this work."

Jen held the door open as they left the cage, carefully securing it behind them.

"Oh yeah, I'm still in, Jen," Sandra said.

"Me too," Janie added.

They followed Jen to the house.

"Good," Jen nodded. "I'm going to need help refining the genetics. How do you feel about in line breeding?"

"I don't know shit about genetics Jen, tell me what to do. I really want to be part of this project," Janie replied.

"My plan is to keep breeding offspring back to their parents until the white gene shows itself more often and becomes more consistent. Can you do that?"

Janie nodded. "Sure. How long does it take for the babies to mature?"

"A year. And then, when the offspring of one line is consistently white we can intermix these lines to lose the bad genes."

"Why bring in the other gliders if you finally have a solid, white line?"

"Too much in-line breeding reinforces other, lesser-known genes to express themselves. Some of these are bad, like the gene that causes elbow dysplasia and hip arthritis in Labradors. All dogs started with the same genes. But, by inline breeding, we focus on a few traits we like and unknowingly bring weaker ones along during the genetic upgrade."

"And...?"

"So, these mistakes should be put down or at least never bred because the bad genes are too strong. They can fuck up the breed, so you must be unrelenting with mistakes Janie."

"I can do that," Janie said. "David will help me."

"Well, you can come over every day if you want. I'm not going anywhere for a long time. I have sugar gliders to raise and a marriage to patch up."

"What's wrong with you and Randy? Is it the sex?" Sandra asked.

Jen smiled uneasily. "Let's go in the house and open a bottle of wine. What kind do you drink? White, I hope?" Jen asked, popping the cork from a chilled chardonnay.

"White's fine, thank you."

"I have a feeling your answer to a lot of things is sex, Sandra," Jen said handing a glass to her and Janie.

"Cheers!" Janie offered. She sauntered off as if she'd rather not hear the conversation, but loitered within earshot, sipping her wine staring out the window.

Jen and Sandra clinked glasses.

"It is if you do it right," Sandra answered.

"You know what I think it is? I've lost Randy because I have too many projects. I've crowded him out of my life and sex gets lost because I'm too busy."

"So, you think its projects?"

Jen nodded. "Yeah, Randy is most responsive to me when we're working together. I've always known our marriage isn't a passionate one, but I'm hoping it can be. I want to recreate the sense of family closeness I felt at the place where I stayed in Australia. I was falling in love with a married man..."

"Really?"

"Yes, he's widowed but married to her memory. So, I'm raising sugar gliders to occupy me in my own home while I attend to my husband. I think it's working."

"What is working, Jen?" Janie asked as she held her glass out for a refill.

"I'm working to become closer with Randy, Janie. He's most responsive when we are both working on a common project. He made the aviary cage, and now I'm helping him design an olive tree orchard.

Chapter 21

Hoof Abscess

Sharing her passion for sugar gliders with Sandra was a wise move for Jen. The ladies' mutual excitement strengthened their friendship. They began taking morning rides together meeting for coffee at Jen's house after which they headed to the stables and check on the sugar gliders making sure they were fed and watered. Also, it was fun to play with them.

With the sugar gliders attended to the women gathered halters and lead ropes. Jen's favorite ride was Candybar the quarter horse mare who was Rory's love as well. Sandra rode an eight-year-old black gelding named Mozart. They saddled the horses and traveled down Jack Creek using one of two main routes. The easiest way was to drop right down into the canyon and head north towards the cemetery. The other way was a shortcut going south along Jack Creek. It went past Victoria's house and stable.

Victoria's pastures were adjacent to Jen's paddocks, and the horses often had snorting and pawing episodes across the fence line when one of them was feeling crabby.

Today they took the route past the neighbor's house. "Hello, Victoria?" Jen called out.

But there was no response. "Hmm, I was going to introduce you. She is usually out with the horses. Maybe; tomorrow. I'll give her a call later today."

They continued past the house and dropped into the canyon at a leisurely walk. It allowed the girls to enjoy a warm sunny morning.

Sandra pointed to the sky. "Do you see those jet trails?" she asked.

Jen looked up. She saw six or seven white trails way up in the sky, contrails or vapor tracks left by the passenger jets on their morning routes between Los Angeles and San Francisco.

"Yes, I see them."

"I have a friend who thinks contrails contain chemicals?"

"Chemicals for what?"

"It's a government conspiracy," Sandra said in a serious tone. "Chemicals are added to the jet fuel by the government!"

"Why would the government want to poison us?"

"Because they want to make us stupid. That way we won't question their authority."

"You're kidding! Aren't you? That's paranoid, don't you think?"

"Well I guess it's working on your friend, then."

They both laughed.

Mozart stopped, whinnied, pulled both front feet out of the muck, and backed up onto the dry area of the bank. As he stepped back, he was limping badly.

"It looks like he hurt his right front foot on something," Jen said.

"Should we keep going? Should I get off?"

"Not yet, let's see if he walks out of it. Go forward four or five steps." Jen said. "Okay now push him further into a trot. See if you can feel a lopsidedness in the gait."

When Sandra prodded him he bobbed his head and changed his gait when stepping on his left front foot to lessen any pain he was feeling in the other foot.

"Okay, stop and dismount, Sandra. I'm going to check it out; maybe he picked up a rock or something."

Sandra bent down right next to Jen.

"Make sure you keep hold of his reins, Sandra, otherwise he'll leave your ass, and we'll have to ride double."

"What do you see?'

"Nothing unusual, some tender spots here on the inside bulb of the heel and here on the medial side of the frog on the bottom."

"They have frogs?"

"Yeah, the bottom of the hoof has a vee-shape, see?"

"Oh yeah."

"Well, that's called the frog. He's probably bruised his foot, that's why he's so tender." She pressed the sore spot a final time causing the horse to pull his leg back. "I think we should call the ride off. We're going to make it worse."

They walked the horses home, to make it easier for Mozart. After unsaddling them, Jen cleaned his hoof but could see no apparent lesions. Deciding to let the horses rest for a day she gave him Bute paste, an oral anti-inflammatory. If he bruised his sole a few days rest was all he needed.

"What's the plan?"

"We'll wait and see. I'll call Rory out if Mozart's still limping tomorrow."

The next morning, he was no better, so Jen called Sandra to cancel their ride.

"Do you want help with the gliders?" Sandra asked.

"Naw let's take a break. Doc should be here any minute, but I'll see you tomorrow."

Jen went to the barn and entered Mozart's stall. He was holding the injured foot up in the air now and hopping on the other three legs. It hurt too much to put any weight at all on the sore foot. Jen haltered him and tied him outside. She filled a black rubber tub with warm water, added Epsom Salts and Betadine liquid and was holding his foot down in the soothing solution when Rory pulled up.

"Oh, you're already soaking his foot. That's good."

She laughed. "I knew you were going to want that Doc."

Rory walked up next to Mozart and leaned into him. Starting at Mozart's shoulder, he ran his hands down the upper leg feeling the elbow and continuing down the foreleg to the knee joint. After palpating the cannon bone above the ankle, Rory moved lower down to the hoof while squeezing the bones to find any sensitive areas and check for possible fractures. He manipulated the joints, the elbow, and the fetlock, flexing and extending each to see if this was where the pain was. He also felt for heat, an indicator of inflammation.

"Oh, here's something interesting," he said when his hand dropped below the fetlock onto the pastern area above the hoof. Placing his fingers on the backside of the pastern he felt a stronger than normal pulse coming from the posterior digital artery. It was throbbing noticeably. "It's in the hoof," he surmised "probably on the inside because that's where I feel the pulse and the heat coming from the foot."

"So, what do heat, tenderness, and a throbbing pulse add up to Doc?"

"Usually it's a cut or puncture in the sole."

He stood up, straightened his back, and went to his truck. Rummaging through the vet pack, he returned with a handful of tools. He laid them on the ground and picked up what looked like a vice grip with a large circular mouth at the end of it. It was a hoof tester. Jen saw it before; a modified pliers with a six-inch bite that allowed Rory to squeeze separate parts of the sole selectively. Mozart flinched when Rory hit the sore spots showing him the problem.

"This helps me diagnose hoof abscesses, laminitis, and navicular disease. See how Mozart responds?" He said as he applied the calipers between the sole and the side of the hoof. The horse immediately flinched and pulled the leg away.

"What is that telling you Doc?"

"Navicular disease causes a horse to flinch when I squeeze the back of the hoof walls, and it may be laminitis if it's tender when I squeeze between the hoof wall and the sole. This is so localized I suspect there either is an abscess or the coffin bone inside the hoof is fractured."

"How can you tell the difference between a bone fracture and an infection?"

"By using a hoof knife. A nice sharp hoof knife will allow me to dig into the sole to look for a puncture hole. If I can't find an abscess, then I'll x-ray it to see if the coffin bone is fractured." Rory squatted down and started digging the round tip of his hoof knife into the painful part of the sole.

"Ah here comes something," he said when the blade exposed a crack in the bottom. As Rory continued to dig, the break started to ooze a putrid smelling fluid. He kept going further until blood began flowing and no more pus came out.

"Yep, it's a simple abscess."

"Then why did Mozart act like he broke his leg?" Jen asked.

"The puncture causes an infection which leads to a throbbing abscess. The hoof wall and sole act like a fingernail barrier. When you hit your thumb with a hammer, the blood builds up under the nail. It's the pressure of the buildup that causes the pain, and it won't stop until a way is opened to allow the ooze to come out. It hurts like hell until I carve a relief pathway through the sole."

"What causes the pus buildup in the first place?"

"When Mozart stepped on something that pierced his sole it left bacteria inside leading to an accumulation of white cells to fight off the bacteria. However, so many white cells come that the liquid inside the abscess expands and gets very painful."

"And soaking helps pull the pus out?"

"Yeah as long as you open an exit hole with a knife." Rory went to the antibiotic drawer in his truck. Dropping some large pills into a brown bottle, he handed it to Jen. "Here Give Mozart twelve of these pills in his grain morning and night and continue soaking his foot for thirty minutes twice a day." To get the healing off to a fast start he gave the horse an antibiotic injection and a tetanus vaccination.

"Can you bill me, Rory?" Jen asked.

"No problem. Oh, Jen, I'll be out of town for a couple of days. I'm driving to Davis. Katie has a break in her schooling. We're doing a mini-vacation in Sacramento. Dr. Osborne is covering my calls."

"Why Sacramento? It sounds boring."

"I'm surprising Katie. We're staying on the Delta King, it's a riverboat permanently moored on the Sacramento River."

"And you can sleep on it?"

"Yeah, they have sleeping rooms available, just like when it was paddling up and down the rivers."

"That sounds romantic."

"That's why I'm doing it. I'm trying to keep Katie in California after she graduates from her MPVM program."

"Okay," Jen smiled. "Have a good time on your little vacation."

Chapter 22

King's Fever

"Good morning Honey," Rory said walking into the office the next morning.

"Hi, Doc. Have you called Doc Katie?"

"Yep, she's cleared her weekend."

"I'm glad, good for her and you."

"Why me?"

"Because you're supporting her going back to school."

"I'm trying to convince her to stay in California instead of working on the reservation. That's why I'm a hundred percent behind her on this MPVM program."

"I don't understand."

"The MPVM program is a two-year course we can take after graduating from vet school. It gives us enhanced training to investigate public health issues. For Katie, the credentials will allow her to take on government jobs just about anywhere, including California."

"Public health issues?"

"Yeah," Rory replied. "Like epidemics and disease outbreaks."

"That doesn't sound like the veterinary medicine I know. Why does she want to go into that field?"

"Katie feels most confident in a regimented job where she works closely with her peers. How's Mozart this morning? Has Jen called?"

"Yep, he's a lot better. Now I have a problem, Doc. King isn't eating, and there's a lump on his face. Can you check him out?" Honey was obviously anxious.

"Sure, bring him back to the exam table. How is he adjusting to his new place?"

"He settled in fine for the first few days, but now he's getting lethargic, and I think he's feverish."

Rory stuck a thermometer in the dog's butt. "Can you hand me the clippers? I'll shave this bump while we wait for the thermometer." He palpated the firm swelling on the right side of King's face right below his ear. "I bet we have a submandibular abscess," he said after shaving and feeling both sides of the head for comparison. "Take his thermometer out. It's beeping."

"Oh, oh. It's 104 Doc."

He nodded. "Yeah, it's probably a lymph node abscess, or it could be cancer. I need to suck up some cells and look at them under the microscope."

That worried her. "Oh, don't tell me King has cancer Doc."

"Shh, it's likely an abscess because he has a fever; tumors don't cause fevers. But the cytology will show me if there is cancer too."

Opening a drawer, he pulled out a syringe with a needle attached. He used a cotton sponge soaked in alcohol to clean the clipped area and poked the needle into the mass, pulling back on the syringe hard enough to suck a sample into it. "It's probably pus. But there sure isn't much. I need to get one drop onto this slide. Oh yeah. Good, I've got it," he said, smearing the sample over the slide with the end of the needle. He held it in the light to ascertain his success.

"Good there's enough here," He could see a small spot on the shiny glass slide. He handed the slide to Honey. "Put this through the Diff-Quick staining solutions to show off the cells better."

"Don't forget to heat-fix the slide first." He reminded her as he handed her the propane torch.

"Why do we need to do this? It seems like I'm cooking the cells. Doesn't the heat hurt them?" She asked as she lit the torch and waved the slide through the flame.

"No, the quick high heat glues the cells to the slide, so they don't wash away in the solutions. It's called heat fixation; we're fixing the cells onto the slide using the flame."

Setting the fixed slide on his microscope Rory dropped his head and focused his eyes through the binocular lenses. "Let's see, lots of neutrophil white cells and some larger white cells with foamy vacuoles in them. This is the result of infection, there are no signs of cancer cells."

"And what does that mean? Do we have to ship King back?"

"To Australia?"

She nodded worriedly.

"No! Honey, why would we do that? It's a simple infection."

That relieved the worried mom. "I'll add an antifungal medicine in case they have something like Valley Fever over there. Now when I come back, I promise to culture and biopsy those lumps if they are not better. Are you okay with that?"

She nodded realizing how illogical she had been in her worry over her beloved dog. "I'm sorry Doc."

"No biggie. You may have a point there, Honey about this dog coming in from Australia." Her concern ignited a nascent worry in Rory. Could the dog have brought something back? "Maybe we should do the full work up right now."

Honey nodded smiling with relief.

"Okay, call IDEXX for a lab specimen pickup. Let's get him sedated and get stuff ready for a CBC, fungal panel, and chem panel. I'll pull more samples and send it in for culture. And finally, we'll biopsy an entire nodule. It's overkill, but it will make both of us feel better, yes?"

Honey smiled and gave him a big hug.

Chapter 23

Dr. Troy

"Answering service for Doctor Evans. How may I help you?"

"This is Jen Bianchi. I need to talk to the Doctor. My gelding is sick."

"Doctor Evans is out of town until next Monday. Dr. Osborne is taking his calls. May I connect you with him?"

"Oh, that's right. He told me he would be gone. Yes, I would like to talk to Dr. Osborne, please."

"Dr. Osborne is on the line."

"Hi, Dr. Osborne, my name is Jen Bianchi, I am a client of Dr. Evans, and I have a sick horse. I think it's colic, but I'm not sure."

"I can come out to see him right now."

Jen gave him directions to her ranch.

"Okay, I'll be there in 30 minutes. In the meantime, keep walking the horse and don't let him drop and roll."

"I thought he would feel better if I let him lie down."

"No, the intestines in a horse can twist on themselves if he drops down and starts to roll."

Jen met Dr. Osborne in front of the barn. He was a compact, muscular man, very freckled, with dark red hair. He walked up to her holding out his hand.

"Hi, I'm Dr. Troy Osborne. You must be Jen."

"Yes. It's nice to meet you. Can I call you Dr. Troy?"

"Fine with me. Which horse is having the problem, Jen?"

"It's Shiloh, a chestnut gelding. Here follow me." Jen took Doc Troy into the arena where Randy was walking the horse.

"Randy come over and meet Dr. Osborne," Jen said. He's recovering from an auto accident," she told the new vet. With his big bandage removed Randy could use the arm for light work but kept it mostly tucked inside a sling.

Dr. Osborne watched the horse for a moment. Every minute or so Shiloh's legs would buckle, and he would try to lie down, but Randy kept pulling on his lead rope to keep him walking. "It sure looks like colic, but I'll have to confirm the diagnosis." Dr. Troy was in the habit of talking to himself, allowing any nearby person free access to his current thoughts. "Let's see; I need a stethoscope, a thermometer, rectal palpation sleeves, and lube. Don't forget the tranquilizer," he remembered while rummaging through drawers.

He walked back to the horse and turned to Jen. "I need to gather some parameters to help me figure this colic out. Give me a minute to get a heart rate, capillary refill time, gum color, and gut auscultation accomplished. After that, I'll give him a tranquilizer, so he won't be as painful."

Shiloh's head was down, and he shifted his weight uneasily. He looked downright miserable and depressed and had an elevated respiratory rate of thirty breaths per minute. The heart rate was elevated to ninety beats per minute, twice what it should be, and the horse was carrying a fever of 103F. Placing his stethoscope on both sides of the flank in the abdominal area to hear how well the guts were rumbling, Dr. Troy heard nothing; the intestines were shutting down. The gums were purple instead of a healthy bright red color, and when Troy pushed his finger onto Shiloh's gums to blanch out the purple color there was a three-second delay before the whiteness disappeared. The horse was going into shock; he needed intravenous fluids immediately.

After giving Shiloh an injection of two painkillers Troy went back to his truck and returned with a bucket, a straight edge razor, tape, suture material, and an 8" long catheter.

"Can you fill this bucket with warm water?" He asked Jen.

He placed cotton batting into the water, squirted the cotton with surgical soap, and soaped up the catheter site. Using his razor, he scraped the hair off the skin above the jugular vein and advanced the large catheter directly into the horse's jugular. This vessel is easy to see; it's an inch in diameter.

Doc Troy knew he was inside the vein when blood rushed back through the catheter. He put a stopper on the catheter's end, placed layers of tape underneath and on top of the exposed part, and sutured the taped catheter into Shiloh's skin to make sure the catheter would not come out. Pulling out a drip set, he showed

Jen how to hold the fluid bag high to allow the life-saving liquid a fast flow into the horse.

This was not a usual colic case where horses become depressed and go off feed when they have a stomach problem. They don't usually develop a fever or a respiratory discharge. Nope, this was not a typical colic case.

Troy put on a long plastic sleeve, covering it with lots of lubrication. He walked to Shiloh's tail, lifted it up, and gently worked his gloved arm into the horse's rectum. Palpation of the four parts of the large colon did not suggest impaction because the ingesta was still soft, like play dough. He pulled out some feces found it was a bit dry but was not so hard as to cause a constipation colic. When he rubbed his gloved fingers together between fecal material he could not feel any grit which would suggest Shiloh had a sand colic from eating feed off the ground.

"I'm perplexed as to the cause of this," Troy told Jen. "It seems to be a combination of colic along with the development of an upper respiratory infection."

"What do you mean?"

"Well, Shiloh has a fever and a runny nose. I don't see these in a regular colic. I'll treat him for colic, but I want to collect samples to see if he has a respiratory virus or bacterial infection. If so he may have pneumonia."

"Okay."

Dr. Osborne pulled blood and put it into two collection tubes. Next, he swabbed the nasal discharge with a sterile culture swab.

After collecting his diagnostic samples, Troy proceeded on with the routine treatment for colic.

To break up any impaction he administered one gallon of mineral oil pumped into the stomach via a nasogastric tube. Jen hated this part. She knew when Doc pulled out his six-foot-long clear hose he was going to put it into Shiloh's nostril.

Sure enough, the vet threaded his clear flexible hose into the horse's left nostril, weaving it through the nasal turbinates to the back of the mouth where he would trick Shiloh into swallowing it into his stomach.

"Once past the head I need to be careful to direct the tube into the correct spot," Troy explained. "Some patience is required at this point. It's important to wait for the horse to swallow. Once that happens, the throat opens up, allowing me to push the tube all the way to the stomach."

"Are the horror stories I've heard true?"

"Probably. A nasogastric tube put into the lungs by accident instead of the stomach is a big no, no. Anything I pump through, water, mineral oil, medicines, will go into the lungs, not the stomach. That'll kill the horse instantly, or close to it."

"So how do you tell? What is your guarantee?"

"I have two of them. First, you watch the tube slide up and down the neck. That means it's in a safe passage, the esophagus. However, if the thing falls into the windpipe, I won't see it move up and down. Second, I puff air into the tube and listen back for a gurgle and wait for bad gut smells. If there is no air push back, I am not in the stomach. Only the stomach fills like a balloon that way."

Dr. Troy made it a point to show Jen the progression of the tube down the neck. "Watch Shiloh's neck right here. Can you see the end of the tube move up and down as I wiggle it inside the esophagus?"

"Yep, I can."

He blew into the tube. The air came whooshing back out, with the bonus of the foul odor of Shiloh's stomach contents. Now with all checks and rechecks covered it was safe to pump in the gallon of mineral oil.

"Why is he panting, Doc?"

"He's not panting he's breathing fast and shallow, probably because his lungs are infected. The painkillers seem to have helped; he's more stable on his feet. I can check his chest out, maybe do a chest tap."

"What will that tell us?"

"It'll give me an idea how much of his breathing difficulty is caused by a lung infection. And if there's fluid we can drain it and run tests on it. Plus, it will help him breathe easier."

"Okay, if you think it'll help. Where do you want him?"

"Bring him into the barn on the concrete. This takes more focus, and I don't want to do it out in the open."

Once inside the barn, Troy handed Jen a large, industrial-sized hair clipper. "Here, take this and shave 1-foot square places on each side of the chest."

"Sure."

111

Troy returned holding a syringe with a big needle attached.

"Yeah, that's good Jen. Now hold his head still." He spoke in a pleasant, conversational tone while he pushed a huge and very long needle into Shiloh's side.

"Why isn't he fighting it?"

"The painkillers, remember? That's why this is a good time to do this." When satisfied of the needle's placement he pulled the plunger, easily sucking a reddish fluid into the clear plastic syringe.

"Yep, here's a big part of the problem. This fluid is building up and stopping his lungs from expanding. Here let me package this sample, and then I want to place a drain. It needs more setup. I'll be right back."

"What will the fluid tell you?" Jen asked, when Troy returned.

"We may pull out some bacteria the lab can grow. Heck, I've found cancer of the lungs this way. But that's an extra benefit. He should become more comfortable as we drain the fluid."

"How much can there be?"

"Two gallons, a whole bucketful can come out of each side. Now it's time for lidocaine, for local anesthesia. A drain's bigger than a needle; he's going to feel me place the drain unless I do this. Jiggle his head while I inject it please, starting now."

Despite the painkillers Shiloh was too antsy to sit still for the procedure.

"Let's put this twitch on him, Jen." Deftly he grabbed the horse's fleshy nose with his hand, quickly replacing it with the vice-like clamp. Jen moved in and took over holding the twitch.

"The area around the lungs is filling with fluid. Ready to do the drain?" He asked her.

"Yep," Jen replied.

Between the sedation and Jen's technique, Shiloh stayed still while Troy made an inch-long incision in the middle of the anesthetized area. He plunged a carmalt, a stainless-steel surgery pliers inside the incision, carefully rotating it back and forth pushing into the pleural space.

"I need to separate the muscle between these ribs, that's why the lidocaine needle is so long."

When he was satisfied he retrieved the drain, a long white plastic tube eighteen inches long, and inserted it between the ribs.

112

Happy with the tube placement, Troy left the carmalts in place, holding both the tube and the carmalts with his left hand. This freed up his right to pull a large syringe from his pocket. He pushed air into the tube with the syringe to inflate a cuff round the end of the drain. The air-filled bubble would keep the surgical drain in place.

"Let's see what we have," he said, as he wiggled the drain, freeing up kinks and clogs. As if someone turned a spigot on, a rush of liquid came from the tube, surprising Troy who lost his grip on it. The tube's end was flung around by the fast-moving fluid spraying onto the floor, flying everywhere, coating everything around it with the liquid from Shiloh's lungs. Thousands of infectious particles splattered hither and yon during the precious moments it took Troy to regain control of the tube.

Luckily Jen was on Shiloh's other side and escaped the shower.

Shiloh started to struggle again. "Whoa, boy," Troy said, as he wiped drops from his face and aimed the flow at the bucket.

"Stop, Shiloh!" Jen exclaimed sharply.

"Shh, softer, Jen, the sedative makes him sensitive to noise. Tell him it's okay while you jiggle that twitch up and down."

"That's a lot of fluid, doc," Jen exclaimed when she saw the bucket fill above the halfway point.

"Yeah, this should help a lot."

Suddenly Shiloh turned his head and pulled the twitch from Jen's hand. It flew across the barn and clattered on the concrete. The horse kicked out and hit the bucket with his foot dumping the blood-tinged fluid onto the concrete where it spread across the surface, spilling into cracks and crevices.

Then the horse turned his head toward Troy, who ducked and fell backward onto the wet concrete. His mouth hung open as he watched Shiloh rip the drain out with his teeth.

Troy was surprised, and shocked. "I think it's time to stop for today," he said. He wiped his sticky hands on his coveralls, grabbed the turned over bucket and picked up the discarded drain. "Make sure you clean the concrete with bleach, Jen. Use one-part bleach to water."

"Why, are you worried?"

"I can't go there, Jen. Let's call it a precaution and take this one step at a time."

"Okay," she said. She could see he was as shaken up as she was.

"We'll do the other side tomorrow." He said as he gave the horse an antibiotic injection. "I'll leave these antibiotic tabs as well."

"Dr. Osborne could this fever be related to King's illness?"

"Who?"

"He's a Queensland Heeler I brought back from Australia and gave to Honey, Dr. Evan's assistant. He's under Rory's care, and he has a fever."

"Well, that would be very unusual Jen, as it would mean it was a cross-species transfer. Make sure you bring it up with Rory, it could make us world famous."

"Famous in a good or bad way, Dr. Osborne?"

Troy flashed a wry smile but didn't answer.

There was little to be done after these administrations, and Dr. Osborne left with his biological samples. "Call me if you need anything more, Jen."

"Oh, I will. Thank you, Dr. Osborne."

Jen had a hard time that night at dinner. Shiloh started acting painful three hours after Troy left and this worried her. Randy noticed her distress. "Is something wrong?"

"Something bad is happening to the horses, and Dr. Evans is out of town. I trust Dr. Osborne knows what he is doing, but I would feel better if Rory were here."

"If Rory left him in charge, he believes in him. Don't stress so much Jen. It makes things worse. I'm sure he will figure this out."

This response was so typical of Randy who stubbornly maintained the point of view that everything eventually works itself out. Still, she waited through the night but called Dr. Osborne for a recheck the first thing the next morning. And now Mozart was exhibiting signs similar to Shiloh's.

"Oh man, I'll get right out there." Troy sighed rumpling his hair. "I'm sorry Jen."

"Me too, this, sucks."

Troy could see they hadn't made any headway with Shiloh. He was walking around aimlessly and bumping into the fence as if he had no sense of vision. Then the horse dropped to the ground, and no matter what they did they could not get him to

114

stand. To make matters worse, the clear nasal discharge was now frothy and tinged red with blood.

"You need to decide if you want to ship him to a hospital, Jen. I don't think I can do much more for him here."

Chapter 24

The Necropsy

Jen made a terrible decision no animal owner ever wants to make. Shiloh's illness was severe enough for him to need hospitalization. Now she must decide whether to send him off or euthanize him. "I've discussed this with Randy," she said. "We need to put him down; we can't justify further treatment costs."

"Are you sure? I can trailer him to the Equine Hospital."

"Yep, I've done this before Dr. Osborne," she said smiling weakly.

Troy filled two large syringes full of a pink fluid. The medication was thick and didn't flow smoothly, so he attached his biggest needles to the syringes. Shiloh was flat on his right side. Walking up behind him Troy placed a knee on the horse's neck. By approaching from the back, he protected himself from injury if the horse flailed his front feet.

Inserting the needle into Shiloh's jugular catheter, Troy squeezed the contents of the syringe into the suffering horse. In a matter of minutes, Shiloh stopped moving and breathing. Now he was at peace.

Troy felt relieved for Shiloh but worried he hadn't diagnosed the problem. He had alleviated one animal's suffering but hadn't done diddly squat for the others.

"We have to necropsy him, Jen. I need more answers."

Jen was still hurting. "Shiloh was doing great; he was in his prime. I've never lost a healthy horse before."

"You can think about a necropsy while we work on the other one, what's his name?"

"Mozart."

Mozart was showing similar signs, and Troy treated him similarly, as a colic case with an attendant infectious process. Jen helped administer meds and gastric oiling.

"We need to necropsy Shiloh, Jen, especially now. We have a second case coming right behind the first."

"What are you thinking?"

"Besides colic, I'm thinking rabies or lead poisoning. The frothy bloody nasal discharge could indicate a respiratory infection such as Equine Influenza or Equine Herpes virus. These possibilities must be ruled out. I have to necropsy get samples to the lab.

"Rabies? Should I be worried?"

"Probably not. It's always up there first on the differential list; it's one of those diseases that are horrible to get. I'm vaccinated, every vet student gets a rabies shot, but we will need to be as careful as we can during the necropsy. It's best if you stay an arm's length from the horse and me."

Cognizant of the mess things turned into yesterday, Troy was much more careful today, fully realizing the potential catastrophe for himself if he became infected. After taking a long, hot, soapy shower as soon as he got home, he had asked Susan to wash everything in a bleach mix, and he sanitized the truck compartments, and any bottles and tools and drawers he used for his call.

Today he was on high alert. He pulled on the long shoulder length gloves used for rectal palpations and then wore a second pair of surgical gloves on top of the palpation sleeve.

Feeling satisfied within his plastic protection barriers, he dug into the dead horse. First, he wanted to look for colic, so he opened the abdomen using a necropsy knife, handling every foot of Shiloh's long intestine searching for a blockage.

"What are you finding?" Jen asked as he pulled and tugged at the intestines and examined the various organs.

"Not much, unfortunately. There is a discolored yellowing of the fatty layer under the skin, and there are splotches of red colored bruising in the stomach and intestinal walls. But I don't see any ugly black area suggesting a gut twist or a death-dealing impaction."

He stopped and stood up. "Can you find a pen and paper Jen? Look in my truck in the front seat. I would like you to write down what I say as I go through this."

"Okay." She returned and nodded that she was ready.

"The ingesta is dry but not enough to cause a blockage." Troy took tissue samples of various organs to send to the lab. "The kidneys and the stomach appear healthy. So, do the small and large intestines, the adrenal glands, lymph nodes, and the bladder."

"How do you spell adrenal?"

"A-d-r-e-n-a-l."

He gathered his baggie of abdominal samples and stood away from the horse.

"Can you open the bag, Jen?"

"The one in your hands?" She didn't want to touch it; it was bloody.

"No, the one in my pocket. Take it out and open it up so I can drop in these samples. I need to regroup. We have to cut the chest open."

She followed him to the truck.

"Why do you have to open the chest?"

"This is more than a simple colic; there's a respiratory component involved. Remember the discharge and the fever?"

She nodded.

"I'm curious to see how extensive the lung problem is."

Troy brought out a large pair of shrub shears. He needed a reliable tool that could break a horse's breastbone and rib cage apart. Jen winced each time the jaws closed on a rib bone, making a horrible crunch.

Pulling the rack of ribs free of the lungs Troy saw a significant amount of fluid pooling between the lungs and the chest wall. This was the pleural space he had drained yesterday. And he noticed small bloody splotchy areas on the outside of the lungs as well as along the chest wall.

"Here comes the messy part." Hacking and plucking the lungs from the horse he laid it out like a butterfly, with the windpipe as its long neck.

"Time to incise down into the windpipe. I need you to hold these culture tubes for me. He walked over and let her grab them from his pocket.

117

"Take two, they're free," he joked. "But, don't open them yet."

"Do I get a surprise?" She asked. She was more at ease now the investigation had begun.

"Only good ones I hope." He continued incising further into the windpipe.

"Ohh, ooh," he said. "This red froth is abnormal, and it gets worse as we dig deeper into the smaller airways. I want you to point one of the tubes toward me with the top my way. Good!" He pulled the top off along with the cotton swab it was attached to and swabbed the tip long enough to absorb a significant amount of sample from the lungs.

"Hold your hands steady. I'm going to push the swab back inside, like so. Okay now label that 'bronchi.'"

She nodded.

"Now give me the others the same way. I want to take a deeper sample. Label this one parenchyma," he spelled it for her. He bent back down over the plucked organs like a kid standing over his Christmas toys deciding which one to open next.

"Oh, wow, look at this pericardial effusion," he pointed out the heart hidden behind lung lobes. The heart sack was filled with a thin bloody fluid, the same color, and consistency he saw around the lungs, definitely abnormal.

She nodded. "What should I call it?"

"Severe pericardial effusion leading to tamponade. Let's get a sample of the pericardial effusion."

"What do you need?"

"A 20cc syringe with a green 1 ½" needle."

"Thank you," he said as he pushed the needle into the heart sac, filling the syringe with the bloody fluid as he pulled the plunger back.

Capping the needle, he dropped the filled syringe into the bag Jen was holding. Next, he incised into the heart muscle and the stretched pericardial lining to get more samples.

After finishing the chest and abdomen, Troy hesitated. "Jen, I want to send the brain to Fresno, but I have to cut the head off. Can I do that?"

"Yes, but I'm leaving. I'll have Randy come with his backhoe. Thank you, Troy. Do you have all the samples? Do you want any more help from me?"

He shook his head.

"Please get in touch with me as soon as you know something. There's so much going on here."

Troy told her he would and returned to finish his work. He located a large knife, and a bone saw in his truck to facilitate the head removal.

Randy drove up in a tractor with a big bucket in front. He turned it off and climbed out to help with the dissection.

"What a mess. What are you doing?"

"I'm removing the head."

"Do you want any help?"

"Yeah grab the nose and jiggle the head back and forth so I can work my knife through a joint." Troy was tired and not thinking. He neglected to advise Randy to wear protective gloves on his hands. "Mother Nature didn't want anyone's head to come off easily."

"Except for moose. A grizzly can swipe a moose's head off."

"Really! Are you sure Randy?"

"Oh yeah. There's a story about a Russian miner hiking through the wilderness who witnessed a moose drinking from a stream, and a Grizzly bear approached from the other side. Moose are very territorial and attack anything they perceive to be a threat to their water source. The moose charged full speed across the stream, and as it neared the bear, the bear stood up and with a quick motion swiped the moose on the side of the face. The moose's decapitated head flew twenty feet."

"Well horses wouldn't lose their heads so easily," Troy decided. "This is a real bitch. Oh, here it comes. Can you open up the big plastic bag Randy?" Troy dropped the massive head into the bag.

"What are your thoughts, Dr. Osborne?"

"Right now, they're way open. I can only think of four things. colic, rabies, lead poisoning, or a virus-like Equine Herpes or Influenza. Where are you burying the body Randy?"

"I was going to dump it on the top of the bone yard. What do you think?"

"That would be all right, but it'll pull buzzards your way for a few weeks."

"It happens every time we lose a cow," Randy said unworried. It was easier than digging a hole for proper burial.

Troy looked around making sure he had all the samples he needed. "Okay, Randy I'm finished here, I'll call as soon as I hear something."

"See ya' Doc."

Climbing into his tractor, Randy started the machine and drove it to the dead horse. He thought it best to scoop Shiloh up by coming at his back instead of his legs and belly. He moved the bucket slowly forward but every time he made contact, with the body he ended up pushing it away. Deciding to approach the corpse from the belly side he positioned the bucket between the legs and slowly pushed the carcass ahead until it was stopped by a retaining wall.

Using the wall as a stabilization method, he continued to push forward until most of the dead horse was in the bucket. With Shiloh's body secured, Randy lifted the bucket in front of him raising the horse high above head level. But when he stopped the upward movement the small tractor shuddered at the sudden stop, and the thousand-pound equine body rocked the scoop back and forth. Suddenly Randy felt liquid falling on his head and face as excess fluid from the chest and belly sloshed out of the bucket sprinkling infectious particles all over him and the ground.

Chapter 25

The Carnage Continues

Jen called Dr. Osborne the next day.

"Mozart is worse as well," she told Troy dejectedly. "He's going the same route as Shiloh."

"Jen, I don't have any lab results yet, so I cannot help you with the diagnosis. Do you want me to come out to see if I can do anything?"

"Yes Goddammit. I wish Dr. Rory was here."

Again, Troy felt inadequate, but he also had a duty to see this through as best he could. He drove back out for the third straight day.

Now Mozart was down and couldn't get up.

"Jen, this is way over my head. We need to get Mozart to Mid Valley Equine Clinic for treatment. Do you have a stock trailer? Because Mozart can't stand, we can't use a regular horse trailer."

"Victoria does. I'll ask to borrow hers."

Jen drove over and hooked up the stock trailer. She drove it back, and Troy, Randy, and Jen pushed and pulled Mozart into the trailer. Victoria's husband John offered to drive the horse. He just came from working out of town and didn't know exactly what was happening, but he wanted to help.

"I'll call the Equine Clinic to let them know what to expect," Dr. Troy told Jen.

The drive to Mid Valley Equine Clinic was futile as Mozart died in the trailer. John checked on him while refueling, found the horse dead, and turned around to bring him back home for burial.

Lab results started to come back, but nothing was positive. Not one of the lab tests showed what the problem was.

Then Victoria called into Dr. Evan's office on Friday. Two of her horses started stumbling around acting like they were blind, walking into fences with their heads tilted. They also had a bloody nasal discharge, which they continually snorted out. The office put her in touch with Doctor Osborne.

"This is a frigging nightmare," he muttered to himself searching his mind for more diagnostics and treatments.

So far, the lab had little information to offer on the cause of the problem. Doc Troy would have to wait for the state lab tests to be finished. He drove to Victoria's ranch, and injected the two horses with the same antibiotics and anti-inflammatory drugs. He didn't have anything else to offer. Other than clear nasal discharge that turned bloody, these two cases were different as Victoria's horses showed little colic but exhibited severe neurological signs.

When Rory arrived home late Sunday afternoon, the answering service gave him the rundown. "Goddammit I hate leaving town," he said out loud. Talking to Jen made him realize something very different and very wrong was happening. His impatience changed to concern. He dialed Troy's number to see what the heck happened while he was gone.

"Answering service for Dr. Osborne. May I help you?"

"This is Doctor Evans. Can you locate Dr. Osborne?"

"He let us know he was going to the doctor. I can connect you to his wife."

"Hi, Susan, this is Rory. What happened to Troy? It sounds as though he's had a hell of a week."

"They think he has a bad case of the flu. He developed a headache, his muscles ache, and he has a sore throat. But when he started throwing up and it wouldn't stop we went to emergency. The doctor sent him home, but the vomiting wouldn't stop, so I brought him back."

"Is he coherent? Can I stop by?"

"I think so."

Rory drove to Twin Cities Hospital and found Troy in bed with an intravenous drip attached to his arm. "Man, you've had a horrible week Troy, what the hell happened?"

Troy began coughing, causing him to be short of breath. "The doctors think I have the flu turning into pneumonia, which is why I have this breathing tube up my nose."

"No, I mean what happened to those horses?"

"I honestly don't know Rory. I cannot put the signs together to make sense of the problem," Troy started another coughing spasm. "And now I have a horrendous headache, and I ache all over. Shoot me now, please."

"What tests have you sent out?"

"I sent blood samples and swab samples to IDEXX for CBC, chemistry panel as well as nasal swabs looking for virus through PCR. I also sent cultures and necropsy samples to Dr. Prasad at the state lab."

"It seems all I can do is Band-Aid the problem while we wait for lab results. I need to get out to Jen and Victoria's ranches. Take care; get well."

Rory drove over to see Jen and Victoria. Because the diagnosis was still unknown, he had few treatment options other than anti-inflammatories and antibiotics. In other words, the only care he could offer was to treat the symptoms, as Troy had done.

As he drove up in front of Jen's barn, he saw Jen and Victoria huddled together in conversation.

"Hello."

"Hi, Dr. Evans. I am so glad you are here," Jen told him. "We've had some horrible things happen while you were gone."

"That's what I gather. I came from talking with Dr. Osborne. He's in the hospital with pneumonia. I went through the cases with him. Until more lab results come back, there isn't much more I can offer. He has done everything I would have done up to this point."

"I don't understand Doc," Victoria complained. "All of the horses are current on vaccinations including rabies. Why can't something be done?"

"Lab tests take time Victoria. Believe me; I want to get to the bottom of this as badly as you do. I'll call both labs and let them know there is a serious problem going on here that remains undiagnosed. The tests that have come back so far are not telling us the actual cause of the problem. The CBC indicates a stress leukogram and the white cell count is low as would occur in a viral infection. The chemistry panel tells us the state of the organs; liver enzymes are elevated, bilirubin is building creating jaundice, and the kidneys are shutting down.

The IDEXX lab is also running a PCR, a polymerase chain reaction test, which looks for actual pieces of viral and bacterial genetic material incorporated into the animal's DNA. In fact, we have a series of PCR tests looking for two types of Equine Herpes Virus, Equine Influenza Virus, and a bacterium called streptococcus equi. The lab is also looking for West Nile Virus.

Right now, I am leaning towards Equine Herpes Virus Type 1 as the cause of this outbreak. The herpes virus can cause neurological signs, and it can also cause respiratory symptoms. There is currently an outbreak of Type 1 Herpes virus here, in California and North Carolina. The California cases have been found not far from here in Bakersfield. The infection causes fever, stumbling, and may progress to partial or complete paralysis."

"When will you know for sure?"

"I put a rush on the PCR test and results should be back tomorrow."

"What else can you do Doc?"

Rory left a bottle of the anti-inflammatory Banamine as well as trimethoprim-sulfa antibiotic tablets to be given to any horse Jen or Victoria felt needed help.

"I have another call right now," Rory said. "Things got crazy while I was away, but I'll be available for you anytime. Don't hesitate to call if you need me. In the meantime, keep the sick horses well away from the others Victoria. I have bad feelings."

"I will Doc," Victoria answered.

Something was bugging Jen, and she couldn't place it. Somehow this was becoming very familiar to her. *Horses are getting sick and dying, and now Dr. Osborne is ill enough to be hospitalized,* she thought. And then it hit her. *Oh God could it be? Could I have brought this back with me from Australia? Is it Hendra? And the dog? Has that even been diagnosed? But how could that be? Carrie said the last case of Hendra was the dog Dusty and that was a long time ago.*

And, Jen reasoned, *I wasn't anywhere near anything that could carry it except at the zoo. But why weren't people getting sick there? It doesn't make any sense. It couldn't be me,* she hoped.

Victoria looked over at Jen. "What are you thinking Jen? "You look terrified."

"I'll ask Honey if lab results are back for King" She grabbed the phone and called Honey.

"Yes, they came in this morning," Honey answered. He has an immunological reaction that we're treating with immunosuppressives."

"You mean he hasn't brought any bug back from Australia?"

"No, absolutely no evidence of infection," Honey answered.

"Wow what a relief. Thanks, Honey. Here, Victoria is making motions to speak to you."

Victoria was very agitated. "It's a virus Honey. I know it is and viruses are aliens. Did you know that?"

"Yes, I know it," Honey agreed. Have you ever seen those pictures they take of them with high-powered microscopes? They all look like spaceships, and those ships are filled with an alien life form that will eventually take over this world. They pop up here and there to let us know that they are in charge and can destroy all of us whenever they want."

"Wait, Honey," Victoria said. "Jen's waving at me. I'll talk to you later." She put the phone down. "What are you thinking Jen?"

"That thing about viruses. If you are right, we can kill viruses with bleach and water. Let's clean and wash the concrete walkways and stall walls, any place we think might be contaminated."

Victoria nodded. She knew something needed to be done. "And we need to isolate the sick horses from the healthy ones," she said. "Could we move the healthy animals out into the back pastures? It would get them further away. You're right; we need to clean the barn. I mean really clean it up, the feeders, the water tanks, and the concrete floor. Let's get the horses out of the stables and clean out the stalls."

Chapter 26

The Diagnosis

The next morning Rory was called out again. One of Victoria's two sick horses went down and would not get up. Again, bloody froth was coming from both nostrils. Rory euthanized the mare with Jen's assistance. After his conversation with Troy he began wearing gloves when treating these horses.

"Where is Victoria?" Rory asked.

"She started vomiting last night. She went to bed early with a headache, and now she feels like shit. What were the lab results for Equine Herpes Virus?"

"They were negative."

"Which means?"

"It means no one has any idea what is causing the problem, Jen. I have ordered toxicology testing at the state lab using samples Dr. Osborne sent in. Maybe there is a weird poison that is common to both of your ranches. IDEXX lab told me they have no evidence for lead poisoning in the blood samples."

Back at the office, Rory put another call into Dr. Prasad's office.

"Hi, Dr. Prasad this is Rory Evans. What are you finding?"

"Nothing concrete Rory, some nonspecific tissue changes on histopath. What did they find at IDEXX?"

"Everything is negative: EHV1, EHV4, Influenza, streptococcus equi and West Nile virus are all negative."

"All right Rory, I'm going to order additional PCR testing for diseases that are not currently in the U.S."

"Don't you think that is a bit of a reach?"

"Possibly but we haven't any idea yet what we are dealing with."

"When will results be in?"

"Tomorrow."

The phone rang the next morning. "Rory this is Dr. Prasad. It's Hendra Virus. The horses are infected with the Hendra virus."

"What is Hendra Virus? It's new to me."

"It has never been found in the U.S. It is a virus from Australia, and it has stayed in Australia until now. This is bad news, Rory. Hendra virus is placed in the Biosafety Level 4 category along with Nipah virus, Ebola virus, and Marburg."

"Ebola? Marburg, holy shit. Those are viruses, humans can get. Is that why it is Level 4?"

"Yes, it can jump from horses, and it kills people. Human infection with Hendra virus has a 50% fatality rate. In infected animals, as many as 75% will die."

"How does the virus infect horses?"

"Urine and fetal droppings from infected flying foxes spread the virus, especially if those droppings land in horse troughs and feeders. Animals become infected when they eat contaminated food."

"Oh no, this is a terrible mess."

"Yes. I'll be calling both the California State Veterinarian and the national USDA Veterinarian in charge of our area to coordinate a rapid response to this problem. In the meantime, do not do any more necropsies without proper training in PPE, Personal Protection Equipment."

"What does that mean?"

"Rory, the virus is in the urine, the blood, nasal discharges, and oral secretions of infected horses. If a person, inhales secretions, or gets fluids on his skin he will become infected. PPEs protect the person handling the horse. They include protective gowns that are impervious to fluids, and filtration masks called N95 masks. They are designed to keep a close seal on the face and prevent viral particles from entering your nose and mouth. Protective eyewear is also required. You can use goggles, protective glasses, or face shields. Finally, you must glove up with surgical gloves that cover the cuffs of the PPE gown."

"What a nightmare. I need to call Katie and see if she can break away."

"Oh, I didn't realize she wasn't with you," Dr. Prasad said.

"She's taking classes with Dr. Schwabe at Davis. I'm sure they'll know of it soon."

"Yes, it's quite a deal. You must take every precaution to make sure you don't become infected," Dr. Prasad reminded Rory. "Also make sure no animals are removed from the property until proper testing of all premise animals is finished."

"What will the tests be looking for?"

"Blood will be drawn and run through tests that look for antibodies against Hendra virus. We're looking for seroconversion; any animal that seroconverts will be euthanized."

"What if a horse seroconverts but recovers? It is now healthy and has antibodies against the virus."

"At this point it's too dangerous to let them live. We don't know anything about this virus. No one knows if the animal's immunity might lapse and allow the virus, possibly hidden within the body, to reemerge."

"What does Hendra do to people?"

"The infection begins like the flu. The infected person develops a sore throat and achy muscles. There is a headache and fever as seen in the flu. If the virus gains a solid footing, the patient develops pneumonia. If it enters the brain, it can cause brain inflammation causing drowsiness, convulsions, even coma."

Rory felt his stomach turn. He had to get the diagnosis to Troy's doctor ASAP. And he needed to get back to Jen and Victoria's places to implement quarantine and isolation measures and tell them how to protect themselves. He immediately dialed the hospital.

"Dr. Osborne has been transferred to ICU. He's taken a turn for the worse Dr. Evans."

"Can you transfer my call to ICU? I need to let the staff know what disease we have here. Please have the doctor in charge of the case give me a call."

Once off the phone Rory put his hat on and drove to Jen's. How was he going to explain something so new so dangerous and so unknown to these people? When he drove up both Jen and Randy came out.

"Did you find an answer?" Jen asked.

"Yep, it's called Hendra virus."

"No, no, no, no!" Jen crumbled to the ground sobbing.

"What Jen? What's wrong?" Rory asked as he helped her up.

"I stayed with people in Australia who lost a family member when Hendra first appeared there. It's a horrible way to die."

"Do you think you brought it over, Jen?"

"I hope not Rory."

"Well, do you feel okay?" He asked.

"Yes, I do."

"And King was the only animal you brought back?"

"Yes," she lied deciding it best to wait. This could turn into a terrible mess, and it could be her fault. She was already on shaky legal ground when she "it's my charm, mygled the sugar gliders into the country.

"Well," Rory said, "Somehow Hendra has come to the Central Coast of California. Because this is such a serious threat, the government has placed Hendra at the strictest biosecurity level they have. The threat of spreading is too much of a risk to take. The California Department of Food and Agriculture is collaborating with the USDA's veterinarian for our area to mobilize personnel to eradicate the problem. They should be here tomorrow. In the meantime, keep all the animals here on the ranch. Don't get close to any sick animal until I obtain protection equipment for us. I need to call Katie; she should be here."

Rory remembered Victoria. "It is very likely Dr. Osborne, and Victoria both have this infection. You must get Victoria to the hospital right now. Let them know she may have the same thing Dr. Osborne has. Troy is currently in ICU."

Jen sent Randy to take Victoria to the hospital while she decided what to do with her sugar gliders. She needed to hide them. They were illegal in California and had to be moved. She called Sandra who had outdoor aviaries she was already remodeling for her gliders. They would have to move all of them over, and they would have to do it in an hour or two.

Chapter 27

Katie Arrives

Rory called Katie, and she called him back an hour later. She'd been alerted to the problem already; it was a big thing.

"Rory, you know you're in the middle of an outbreak?"

"I figured that."

"I'm coming down with Dr. Fowler. We're setting up a crisis center at the Mid-State Fairgrounds. Dr. Prasad is on his way with a team from Fresno. Don't touch anything until I can teach you the right way to wear a PPE suit. We will be showing people the way to dress and wear them at the center. You can't go near any contaminated place without this gear. We should be there in six hours."

"What will they do with the places that are contaminated?"

"The ranches that are affected will be cordoned off with yellow tape and armed guards will be there to stop people from coming near. This part is happening right now, and law enforcement has been notified."

Rory met Katie and Dr. Fowler at the fairgrounds that afternoon.

"You remember Rory Evans don't you Dr. Fowler?" Katie asked. Rory is my fiancé."

"Yes, mostly downstairs, large animal," Dr. Fowler said shaking Rory's hand. "It's not the best time to meet, is it?"

"I'm worried to shake hands," Rory admitted.

"Don't go near the barn, the horses, or the dogs without gloves and a mask and don't touch anything unless you're wearing a PPE suit," Katie said.

"You also have to wear these white muck boots if you walk onto the property past this point," Dr. Fowler said pointing to several pairs of waterproof boots. "I've brought plenty. You should take a pair."

"Thank you, Doc," Rory said. "Maybe it's best not to go in," he conceded.

"Let the hazmat crews work through this mess," Dr. Fowler concurred. "Katie, we need to make sure the local hospital has facilities to deal with a Biosecurity Level 4 threat. Have you been in touch with the doctor's there?"

"Yes. Dr. Osborne and two others have been moved from ICU into a separate biohazard isolation room."

"Can you call the hospital for an update, Katie?"

Nodding, she dialed the phone. "Hi, Dr. Perrone, this is Dr. Katie Reynolds. I'm with Dr. Evans, a veterinarian here in the north county. Two of our clients' ranches are being quarantined because the state lab has diagnosed the presence of Hendra Virus in the horses here. The state veterinarian coordinating the process wants to make sure you can verify the Hendra diagnosis."

"We do not have the capability or the licensing to diagnose Biosecurity Level 4 agents. Those samples are sent to another lab. But if the diagnosis of Hendra virus is confirmed there is little to be done treatment-wise, other than offering supportive care in the way of IV fluids, oxygen, and anti-inflammatories. Antiviral medications tried during the Australian outbreak did not help control the Hendra infections."

"Oh, you have heard of this," Katie was surprised. She was glad the word traveled so quickly, and more health professionals were coming on board. "You mean to tell me, Dr. Perrone, there is nothing we can do medically other than supportive care even if we have a verified diagnosis?"

"That's correct."

"Then how do we control this disease?"

"First we have to stop the spread among the horses with euthanasia and cremation or proper burial techniques. And we have to find out how the virus got here. So far in Australia, there has only been viral transfer from horses to people. Individuals with Hendra haven't infected others yet. At this time the viral cycle seems to stop at humans. If that changes, we are going to have a gigantic epidemic. Therefore, we are taking no chances and will impose strict quarantine measures on the patients in isolation."

"Okay, I'll let the men up here know this."

Later that morning two sheriff's cars drove to Jen's house. One stopped at the beginning of the drive where two deputies put up roadblocks at both her and Victoria's driveway. The other vehicle drove, to the house. It was Sheriff McKissack and another fellow.

"Hey John," Jen said. They had known each other since middle school and went through two quick and failed relationships before giving up that sort of thinking. John was handsome and tall with smooth black hair, dark eyes, and a quick wit. He was the youngest sheriff in recent memory, and now he was anxious. Sheriffs are elected, and he wanted to prove his worth to his constituents.

A tall man with white hair came from the passenger side. He was holding paperwork on a clipboard.

"Hello, I'm Dr. Fowler, and I head the Animal Health Branch for the State of California. Dr. Prasad informed me there is an outbreak of Hendra on this property. May I have some time with you?" he asked Jen.

"Absolutely."

"This virus has only been found in Australia. Have you traveled there?"

"Yes, earlier this year I escorted one of my dogs through quarantine. I stayed six weeks."

"Did you bring any animals home?"

"Yes, I brought King over, he's a Queensland Heeler. He's under Dr. Evans' care for an immune thing unrelated to Hendra or anything from Australia. His receptionist owns him now. She might not want to talk though because she doesn't trust the government. But other than having two bumps removed he's been fine, ask Doc."

"We need to take blood from all the animals you have on the premises. And we have to see any humans who could have been exposed to this virus."

"What happens if a positive test occurs?

"We'll discuss that when and if we need to. I also need you and your neighbor to let us know if there are any animals you have taken off the ranch."

"Only King the Heeler, the one with the bumps. Oh, and my Chesapeakes. Honey takes them out for bird dog training."

"Are there any other people on the ranches?" Dr. Fowler asked.

"Victoria's husband John has been working out of town. Randy, my husband, is in the house. He hasn't been feeling well, so he's in bed today."

"Get him to the hospital immediately. You should go right now; the medical teams have arrived. Which hospital will you be at?"

"Twin Cities, I guess."

"Okay, I'll call ahead. Both you and your husband need to be tested. We have to see who is carrying this virus."

"What kind of tests?"

"Blood and throat cultures."

Jen didn't leave right away. She wanted to see what the crews were going to do. While she and the Doctor were talking two trucks drove onto her property. Three men exited each vehicle and went immediately to the utility packs in the back of each truck to don white, whole body suits with hoods. They also wore long rubber gloves, rubber boots, and full-face respirators with filters. As they helped each other gown up Jen noticed the care they took to make sure there were no breaks in their protective gear, following the buddy system to check the other as they clothed. They taped the tops of the gloves and boots to the suits. They even taped the front zippers. Jen suddenly felt exposed and vulnerable. She followed behind one group and her presence was not an issue, so she stayed in the background to watch.

Working in trios the men went from horse to horse drawing blood samples. Another group focused on the dogs.

Dr. Fowler saw that Jen hadn't left and continued his questioning. "Where did you dispose of the dead horses?"

"We have a bone yard in a small canyon at the far end of the property."

"Either bury the dead animals in a deep trench, or you can cremate them where they are. They cannot be left above ground unless they are thoroughly cremated. This property is quarantined, which means no animal movement is allowed on or off the ranch until the order is lifted."

"How long will quarantine last?"

"One cycle of Hendra virus replication and spread requires sixteen days. The Australian government lifts quarantine after there are no more positive results at the end of two Hendra cycles, which is 32 days."

It suddenly hit Jen that Randy could be in real danger. "I think I should get Randy to the hospital," She said hurriedly. "I'm anxious about him."

"As well you should be," replied Dr. Fowler. "What is your cell phone number in case I need to find you?" She rattled off her number and walked to the house to take Randy to Twin Cities.

She waved to the deputy guarding the quarantine area and watched him pull down the Do Not Cross yellow tape, letting her leave her ranch.

"Wait here, Randy I'll let them know who we are," she said after parking in the emergency area.

Soon Jen returned with an orderly pushing a wheelchair. He had on a facemask and rubber gloves. He helped Randy into the chair and moved him directly to an isolation room. Jen didn't have time to change into isolation garments, so she blew Randy a kiss goodbye and told him she would be back later.

Then she went to the front desk of the emergency ward. "My name is Jen Bianchi. I wheeled my husband, Randy into isolation with a possible, Hendra Virus infection. Dr. Fowler requested I submit lab samples. Who is coordinating this?"

Chapter 28

Jen is Alone

After her own tests were done Jen walked to the isolation area. Rory was already there, as well as Troy's wife, Susan who was sobbing in Rory's arms.

"What happened?"

"Troy passed away from pneumonia early this morning," Rory said.

Jen started shaking. "What about my husband? What about Victoria?"

"She's okay so far. IV therapy will give her the edge they need to fight this thing," replied a nurse near the group.

"Why did Dr. Troy die in spite of your excellent IV therapy, then?" Jen asked, irritated.

"It all depends on how many infectious particles a person is exposed to. Evidently, Dr. Osborne was too close to the situation for too long. His body could not kick out the infection even with support."

Jen was unnerved as well as angry. There would be no guarantee Randy or Victoria would be coming home either.

"Can I see my husband?" Jen asked the nurse.

"Yes, but I need to show you how to wear a PPE suit. You'll also need to wear a mask, and if you want to touch the patient, you must have gloves taped to the sleeves of the gown."

Jen's mood darkened as the nurse assisted her in putting on the protection suit. *I need to get past this. I need to be there for Randy*, she thought. Jen put her chin up, smiled, and walked into the isolation room ignoring the monitors and the tubes attached to Randy "Hi, baby. I miss you," she said through her forced smile.

"I miss you too, dear. How are things back home?"

"The same; no significant changes."

"Oh, good. I thought this was going to blow up into a nightmare."

Jen didn't want to burden him with the reality of the situation. Randy was fatigued and not always coherent. She sat with him for a long while. At times, he dosed off and woke up complaining of head and muscle aches. Periodically, a nurse would come in to check his lines and monitors. After a few hours, there was a knock at the inner door.

Jen rose to open it a crack and saw Honey.

"Hi, Jen," Honey announced. "Victoria seems okay right now, and I wanted to see if you need something before I leave."

"How is she doing?"

"Hanging in there, but she's never off the pain meds long enough to get through the stupor."

"How did you do with all the questions?" Jen asked her.

"I did fine. I didn't have much to say. They wanted to know about King, and what I knew of the animals at your place."

"Did you tell them about the sugar gliders?" Jen asked worriedly.

"No, I was more focused on our dogs and horses. I'm going home for a few hours, Jen."

"I'm staying here, I'm not ready to leave Randy Please don't say anything about the gliders."

"No problem. I can't hug you because I took off my suit. I'll see you later."

"Where's Sandra?"

"She left an hour ago. She's home."

"I'll stay with her. I can't go back home, Honey. There is way too much shit going on here. I need a break," Jen started to cry.

"I understand, Jen. I'll take care of feeding tonight. You need to take care of yourself," Honey said.

"Don't forget to feed Victoria's horses. No one's there right now. John won't leave the hospital until Victoria is better."

"Okay, Jen."

Because of Randy's frequent naps, Jen had lots of time to think. She was not used to sitting still, doing nothing. However, right now it didn't matter because wherever she was, she would be sitting and staring, or wandering and wondering why she had shredded her life to pieces. *I may as well be here for Randy,* she thought. Jen put on gloves and taped them to the sleeve of her gown. She reached over and gently held Randy's hand for a long time. Everything she had working for was being destroyed.

Hours later Jen heard another knock. It was Honey again.

"The nurses told me you're still in here, Jen. I've gone and come back already."

"Hang on, Honey, it's time for me to take a break anyway. Let a nurse know I need help removing my protection suit."

A few minutes later Jen was stripped of her life-saving outfit. She walked over to the nurse station with Honey. "You got back quick," she said.

"No, you must have fallen asleep in there. It's quite late. I've talked with Sandra, and she's expecting you, Jen," Honey said. "You should go. I've taken care of the dogs and horses so give yourself a break, hang out with Sandra."

Honey took Jen in her arms and held her. "Get out of here; we've got this, Jen."

Jen drove to Sandra's place.

"I'll be right there!" Jen heard Sandra yell out.

The door opened. "Hi Sandra," Jen said. "Is it okay if I stay here tonight? There is too much stuff going on at my house."

"No problem Jen. I was expecting you. Can I get you something to eat?"

"No, I'm not hungry."

"How about something to drink?"

"Okay."

"What would you like?"

"I don't know, whatever you're having."

Sandra put her arm around her. "Then we'll drink to commiserate. Jen, give yourself a break. You need to relax, try not to obsess on the situation."

Jen looked at her in disbelief. "People are dying, and you want me to relax?"

"Jen, the things that are happening are supposed to happen. We can struggle and fight it, or we can accept the fact. This is how life is; there will always be setbacks."

"I think you have your head in the sand, Sandra. I feel differently. It seems like I caused a car accident that is killing my husband and my neighbor."

"Do you think the gliders brought this over, Jen?"

"Nope, that's impossible. I asked Carrie. The gliders don't carry the Hendra virus."

Jen appreciated the numbing effect of the wine. "Thanks," she said after a while. "That was exactly what I needed. One more glass and I'm ready for bed."

Jen slept in late. Exhausted, she needed rest. She was awakened when the door creaked open.

"Honey called from Dr. Rory's office, Jen. There's an official meeting at ten at your ranch this morning."

Jen sat up. "Oh, I haven't fed my animals!" she realized.

"Not to worry. Honey told me to let you know she and Tal fed this morning. Be there by ten."

Jen arrived to see Rory's truck in front of the barn. She drove up behind him and parked. Rory came from the driver's side, and Dr. Fowler came out the passenger door.

"Good morning," Dr. Fowler said. "Some of the animals on this property have tested positive for the Hendra virus, Mrs. Bianchi."

"What does this mean?"

"They will have to be put down, and their bodies disposed of."

"Can I see your paperwork?" Jen scanned the lab results. "You only have numbers here; they aren't even named. Are you sure these are the correct animals? You don't even know their names," she said, holding the paper with shaking hands.

"We placed microchips inside every animal when we tested them. That way there will be no mistaken identity problems."

"Which animals are they?" Jen asked.

"There is a black mare on your property, and there are three horses next door."

"I call the black mare Midnight. What about the dogs?"

"All the dogs are negative."

"How do you think the infection got here then?"

"We still think it was from the dog you imported from Australia, the Heeler."

"But he showed up negative! His fever was from an immunological disorder. Dr. Evans ran multiple blood tests on him. We even sent in biopsies of bumps on his skin. We already looked for Australian bugs. We didn't find any! He's been healthy since we put him on the cyclosporine and pred pills!"

"Still we think he introduced the virus here, but seroconverted afterward, for some reason."

"You think King carried the virus from Australia and gave it to the horses, but cleared the infection himself?"

"Yes, although it is speculative. There has been no documentation that Hendra can be spread from infected dogs, but we can find no other reason for this virus to have made its way into our area. We're going to have to euthanize him as well."

"You mean you're going to put King down?" Jen erupted in anger. "Are you going to burn my house down too? King is a sweet boy. He hasn't done anything wrong, and he hasn't been sick. I really, really resent your assumptions."

"The euthanasia decision is out of my hands. Hendra virus is too damaging to assume that this negative blood reaction is not significant. I'm sorry."

"When will the animals be put down?" Jen asked quietly.

"Two teams are on their way over right now. You must hire a large backhoe and begin digging the graves."

"Why the hell don't you find a backhoe? You're the one who's killing my animals!" Jen walked away so they would not see her crying. She went into her house to find her neighbor Tom's number. His backhoe was a lot larger than the small tractor Randy used.

"Tom, this is Jen. I need a favor."

"What is all the yellow tape around your driveway for, Jen?"

"That's why I need your help, Tom. The government has found a new virus on the property. They are going to euthanize the infected animals, and I need to bury them."

"Jen, does it affect humans? I want to help you, but I don't want to get sick."

"Yes, but there are safety procedures already in place. The government people have protection suits for you to wear, and they will help you disinfect the tractor once you are finished."

"Okay. When do you want to do this?"

"Can you drive over in your pick-up? You and Dr. Fowler can discuss the plan. Be straight with him. Don't assume anything and don't try to do it your way. Listen to how they want this thing done, and you will be at minimal risk.

"Will you be there, Jen?"

"No, I can't bear to watch this and Randy's in the hospital. I need to be with Randy"

"Randy is sick? Is it this virus? Are you sure it's safe for me?"

"There are several people working here right now, and they are fine. Do exactly as they tell you, okay? Ask for Dr. Fowler; I'll tell him to expect you."

Jen drove back to Twin Cities. Changing into her isolation suit, she went through the double door security into Randy's room.

Randy was worse. He was barely coherent as he slid in and out of consciousness. Jen pulled up a chair, took his hand, and felt his body trembling. She pushed the button to summon the nurse. After a few minutes, one entered the room in an isolation suit. She went through the tubes, drip lines, and monitors to make sure everything was working correctly. "He's starting to shake," Jen told the nurse. "Is there something the doctor can give him?"

The nurse filled a syringe of clear fluid. She injected the solution into the drip line until the tremors abated. Pulling the syringe from the side port, she emptied the remainder into the into the bag of fluids steadily dripping into Randy's vein.

"What is that?" Jen asked.

"Diazepam, valium. It calms low-level tremors."

"Thank you."

After the nurse left Jen took Randy's hand again. All she could do was wait. *I could pray*, she thought. *Pray? Pray for what? Pray to the Almighty God to let him know how humbled I am because He has seen fit to destroy everything in my life? Why would He pick me out? Is there a lesson to be learned here?*

Jen thought not. There was no sense to this. She had lived her life as honestly as possible. Where did this malevolence come from? As she sank into depression, she became inconsolable.

Jen remained by Randy's side for another two hours. Slowly, the tremors returned as the Valium wore off. As time went on the tremors became more severe, soon developing into whole body seizures. Jen pushed the call button. The nurse returned and called the front desk. The doctor in charge came in. He was carrying another syringe, which slowed Randy's jitters way down.

"What is that drug?" Jen asked.

"Phenobarbital."

"How long will it help?"

"We're not sure. It depends on how inflamed the brain is."

"What causes the brain inflammation?"

"Once the Hendra virus gets a foothold inside the brain it has unlimited access to the entire central nervous system. The inflammation it causes disrupts standard electronic signals, effectively short-circuiting the brain."

"Is it curable?"

"The longer the virus lives inside the central nervous system, the less chance he has of a recovery."

Suddenly the room became small, and the suit was stifling hot. Jen was dizzy and began to sweat. "I need to get some air," she said as she opened the door and left the room.

Randy's dying, Jen told herself, *and there is nothing anyone can do about it*. She called Honey. "I need you to pick me up. I'm at the hospital, I can't drive right now."

"I'll be there in thirty minutes."

Honey brought Jen home. "I want to be near my dogs, Honey. They are the only things I have left."

"Do you want me to stay with you?"

"No, I want to be with my dogs."

"Okay, let me know if you need me."

Jen walked through the front door and straight to the garage. She let her Chessies in the house and sank to the floor, sobbing. At first, the dogs were happy to see her, competing for closeness and attention. However, Jen did not respond. She remained on the floor with tears running down her face. This puzzled the dogs. They were not used to this new form of behavior. They quieted and plopped on the floor next to her.

Jen was beside herself. She needed to talk to somebody who understood. Sandra didn't seem to comprehend the depth of this tragedy. She believed in this karma thing that Jen could not accept. *Oh well, we all have our own way to cope*, Jen thought.

Suddenly Jen thought of Carrie. They had stayed in touch during with emails, and phone calls. Carrie would understand. She lived through this herself. It was ten in the morning in Brisbane. Carrie was on her sales rounds and pulled the car over when her cell rang.

"G'day, this is Carrie."

It was so good to hear Carrie's voice. "Carrie, this is Jen."

"Jen! How wonderful. I was just thinking of you. I posted a long letter showing how well Pounder is coming along. You would be so proud. He's the best dog, and Mum loves him so. What's up with you, Hon?"

"Carrie, something awful has happened here."

Carrie was immediately concerned. "Jen, are you okay? You sound terrible."

"Randy is dying," Jen sobbed. "Carrie, he's infected with Hendra virus. Right now, they're keeping him heavily sedated. Otherwise, he develops seizures."

Carrie was silent for a long time. "Hendra? Are you sure?" she finally asked in a small voice.

"Yes. They have quarantine the ranch, and have euthanized my horses, as well as the Queensland Heeler I brought back with me. They also euthanized my neighbor's horses. Randy isn't the only person infected. My next-door neighbor and the vet who necropsied the first horse went to the hospital. The vet died a few mornings ago. They think the virus came over with the Heeler. Oh, Carrie, it's all my fault." Jen broke down crying again.

"Oh my god, Jen. How could that be? There is no Hendra outbreak here right now. The pup's kennel is clean, I'm sure. Did they find the virus in the dog? That's rare; it's happened only once."

"No, he came up negative. Still, they think he brought it over, and somehow cleared the infection temporarily from his bloodstream. But he may be something they call an intermittent shedder, and they don't want to risk the possibility of a recurrence."

"That's why Mum remains angry to this day. They come barging in and do what they want with your life."

"I haven't been able to eat or sleep for days now. If I lose Randy, I don't think I can bear to come home anymore. In fact, this is the first time I've been home in three days. I'm staying at a friend's house right now, but she doesn't need this. Carrie, could you come here to be with me? Could you get away?"

Carrie was silent for a minute. "The first thing you must do is leave your home. Not forever, but until you can feel relaxed in it again."

"I'm doing that. I'm doing exactly what you say. But I also need you here, Carrie. Please, please come out. I will cover the costs. I know that it's a lot to ask," Jen hurried on. "I wouldn't ask if I didn't need you. I need someone who understands."

"Believe me, Jen. It's not that I don't want to be there for you, but it scares me to even think of walking into that again. I left a job I loved because of it. I saw my best friend die because of it. I know how devastating it is. And you don't ever know where it came from or where it's hiding right now. Because it just is, you know? It never really goes away. It's waiting." Carrie paused.

"I probably sound paranoid to you," Carrie said.

"Oh, no. I understand why you are hesitant to come here. But they have completely scoured our barns. They have buried all the animals that were infected. Besides that, I could rent another place somewhere. We don't even have to be near where it happened. I need you so badly," Jen pleaded.

"What about your dogs?"

"Honey will take care of them. She doesn't seem to be bothered staying here. Please, Carrie. Would you think about it? Come for a while."

"Okay, I'll try," Carried acquiesced. "I'll see how much time I can get off and call you back. I'm sorry I said no, Jen. It frightens me so."

"Oh, thank you, thank you. Please call as soon as you can. I love you, Carrie. You don't know how much this means to me."

"I think I do, Jen. I'll call you very soon. I love you too, sweetheart. Keep it together, luv, I'll be there soon."

"Wait, Carrie, one more thing. Is there any evidence that sugar gliders carry Hendra?"

"It has not been found to be so."

"Okay. I'll be waiting for your call."

During the drive home, she began to count the guide posts on the road. One, two, three, one two three, her comforting mantra kept a panic attack at bay. "I have to be able to drive." She thought as she tried all her known methods of self-calming.

Jen hung up, picked herself up off the floor, and wandered around the house. The dogs were quietly milling around her wagging their tails. They were content because their master was with them right now. Jen, however, found little solace in her beloved dogs. All she could feel was emptiness and loneliness.

A knock at the door pulled Jen from her thoughts. Two SLO Sheriff deputies were there.

"Can I speak to Jen Bianchi?" one asked after sahe opened the door.

"I'm Jen."

"I'm sorry to tell you this, Mrs. Bianchi. Your husband has passed."

"Randy died?" She asked tearfully.

"Yes m'aam."

Jen crumpled to the floor.

Chapter 29

Final Goodbye

Early the next morning knocking on the door woke Jen from an exhausted sleep. She opened it, surprised to see two sheriff deputies.

"Mrs. Bianchi? Can we come in? We have sad news."

Jen trembled as she opened the door and let the men in.

"Your husband died at Twin Cities Hospital this morning."

The deputies stood solemn and stone-faced. Holding herself together, Jen nodded.

"Dr. Perrone asks you call him at this number," one said handing her a card.

"Is there anything else we can do for you?" The other man asked softly after a minute.

"No, thank you," Jen replied, "I'll call in a few minutes."

This is Dr. Perrone. We have to confirm the cause of your husband's death, and I need your permission for an autopsy."

"Do I have to give my permission?"

"Jen, they are going to do the procedure with or without your permission. I was calling to let you know this is our next step. They shipped Randy's body to a biosecurity level 4 lab in Colorado. After they collect samples, they will cremate his body, and send the ashes back to you."

"Oh, God," Jen started to cry again. "They've already taken him?"

"It will be okay Jen. His ashes will be back here tomorrow or the next day at the latest. Do you have anybody there with you? Can I call someone for you?"

Jen composed herself when she heard the worry in his voice. "I'll be alright. My friend Honey is here. She takes care of the place when I'm gone and babysit me when I'm home. I'll be all right. Thank you for your concern, Doctor."

"Where do you want us to send the remains?"

"I'll call as soon as I have made arrangements. Thank you, doctor."

Jen wandered the empty house sobbing. Not knowing what else to do she drew up a steamy tub of bathwater, filling the tub Randy installed for her. She always did her best thinking in the tub with a glass of wine.

She went to the kitchen for some chardonnay. Returning to the bath she set her glass down. Disrobing, she slid into the warm liquid cocoon and poured her first glass. Between the warmth of the tub and fuzziness of the wine, Jen began to relax, and the walls erected around her pain started to come down.

She thought of Randy as she sat in the bath. The tears started up again. "So, this, is it?" She cried out. "This is all that's left of Jen and Randy? A memorial service and that is the end of our lives together?"

Jen was sadder than she could remember. She had tried so hard to recover their relationship, and now the whole thing was gone forever. It was something she was unprepared for, something she didn't know how to accept, something so devastating there was nothing left for her at all. This was so unfair.

"Why is it, other people are so content in their lives, and why was it that you and I couldn't even take a trip together?" Jen asked Randy "Spending quality time is a decision, not an accident. For you, there was always something else going on! You never put us first."

She started to cry again. "I wanted so much more for us. Oh God, how do I go on?"

After her second glass, the water had cooled, so she stepped out and dried off. "I'll keep going. That's all I can do. I'll put my head down and keep moving," she decided as she cinched her robe.

Randy's ashes arrived at a funeral home in Paso Robles the next day. Two days later Jen hosted a memorial service for friends and family. Honey took her in hand and steered her through the memorial and subsequent internment in a mausoleum at the cemetery. Everyone was in shock at Randy's death, and very worried for Jen.

She stumbled through the following days in a haze, eating little and trying to sleep when Honey told her to. Eventually, the pain faded, and she started to come back to life. Responding to Honey's ministrations, she found herself looking forward to calls from Carrie. Billy even called to offer his condolences. With his cajoling and Carrie's adventurous spirit, the brother and sister set a date for Carrie's flight to San Francisco. Jen readily focused on that.

Victoria gradually improved and survived the infection, but she was seriously debilitated. With medications, she was able to walk a few hours a day, but could no longer ride or maintain her horses, and would never return to her ranch work.

Jen felt uncomfortable in the house she had shared with Randy and told Honey she could stay in it while Jen moved over with Sandra. She left with nothing but a few clothes. Everything else she left behind. Even her dogs stayed behind because they were still under quarantine.

Her animal ardor severely diminished, Jen went for long walks along quiet hillside trails, on some of the same trails she previously rode her horses. She even neglected her new pets, the sugar gliders, who were quietly reproducing in the aviary behind Sandra's barn.

Jen's walks were the only things she did. Everything had become pointless, flat. However, she marked her calendar, circling April 10 in loud red ink, and each day she would put an X in the present day, so she could see how much longer she had to wait for Carrie. She had blocked out two weeks of Xs before she realized Carrie was due in another week. That perked her up. Not wanting to bother her with phone calls, Jen sent her daily emails to keep in touch. She knew Carrie would be busy arranging her affairs and tickets and passport for her visit.

The morning the X's met the circle was like Christmas for Jen. She was humming and vibrant as she readied herself for the trip up to SFO to pick up her Australian friend. Jen called the airline, and the flight was on time. She wanted to show Carrie San Francisco, as Carrie had shown her Brisbane.

Jen was waiting outside the customs area for Carrie. The two women hugged a long time, and both began a happy cry. Theirs was a very elite club whose common interests were solidified by the horror of Hendra. They were unwilling participants in a macabre society, whose close family members vanished because of some incomprehensible whim of an unseen killer. Now they were closer to each than many sisters would ever be.

Chapter 30

Carrie Arrives

Jen decided they would stay in San Francisco a few days. This was Carrie's first trip to the United States. Sydney had always been compared to San Francisco, and Carrie was eager to see some of this beautiful city. During the days they visited Fisherman's Wharf, the Strybing Arboretum, and the Presidio at Golden Gate Park. At night they found restaurants suggested by the concierge at the hotel and ate until they were stuffed. It was exactly what Jen needed. It took her completely away from the horror at home.

They spent the next two days taking a leisurely drive down Hwy 1, stopping at the Monterey Bay Aquarium, and an outdoor lunch at Nepenthe's overlooking the Pacific Ocean. Jen booked them a room at San Simeon so that they could be included in the earliest tour of Hearst Castle the next day. Jen took Carrie wine tasting along Hwy 46 as they turned east from the coast to get into Paso Robles. They stopped in Paso for dinner, and finally decided that they had had enough fun. It was time to get home. They arrived at Sandra's house late in the evening and went directly to bed. Jen fell into a deep, exhausted, dreamless sleep.

The next day Jen awoke, and stepped out of her bedroom to see Carrie already fussing in the kitchen.

"Hey Jen. How are you today?"

"I think I'm ok. I was so tired and slept so soundly I'm in kind of a fog right now."

"Where are all of your dogs, Jen? I fully expected to see them running this place! You made such a fuss about keeping them with people all the time. So, where are they?"

"They're with Honey Rose. She lives in a little house at the front of the property. She lost King to Hendra. She's glad to have the other dogs around her."

"But what about you? I never imagined you without your dogs."

"I'm not really without dogs. It's just that I don't want to think about any of that for a while. And, because Honey takes such good care of them, I haven't had to. Also, it wasn't until four days ago when quarantine lifted that animals were allowed to move on and off the property."

"So how about we get them over here? I have fallen in love with Pounder, and I would love to meet the rest of his family."

"Ok, I guess I'm ready," Jen said hesitantly. "Let me call Honey."

Honey arrived an hour later with dogs hanging out all of the windows of her car. When she opened the door, they tumbled out and ran in a rush to Jen. It was almost more than she could do to stay standing. She shouted a command. "Down!" All the dogs immediately sat down, looking at her, their tails wagging ferociously.

"Carrie, I would like you to meet Jocko, Pounder's sire," Jen said as she pointed out the dark chocolate colored male. "This little lady here," Jen pointed to a smaller female, the same color as Pounder, "Is Junebug, Pounder's dam. The dun colored female is Lucy, a sister from Pounder's litter, and the pale chocolate male is Preacher. He's from the litter before Pounder's."

"I am so glad to meet you," said Carrie, as she patted each of them. "You're all so well behaved! Oh, they're beautiful, Jen, just beautiful. I can see why you like this breed so much."

"This was a good idea," smiled Jen. "I'm glad you pushed me."

"It's about time someone did," Honey laughed. "This is the first time I've seen you smile in weeks."

"Let's go out to the lake, and let the dogs have their running and swimming time. They haven't been out for a long time, have they Honey?"

"No, too much bad Karma. I felt it unwise to let them wander when the vibes were so unfavorable." Jen and Carrie shared a quick glance with one another.

The gaggle of six human legs and sixteen dog legs started slowly towards the small lake. As the dog's excitement increased, they pulled out in front of the people, and everyone could walk their full stride normally. Jen showed the group her favorite spot.

It was off a point surrounded by water on three sides. Jen had brought sticks, and Honey tennis balls. The dogs overwhelmingly preferred to retrieve the tennis balls. Staying low in the water the sticks were not as easy to see. Colorful tennis balls, on the other hand, bobbed up and down on top of the water.

The dog's retrieved the balls from the water for at least a half hour. It was great fun watching them exercise. Slowly, the energy level dropped. It was time to bring the dogs home.

Chapter 31

Montana De Oro

"How do you feel about riding horses?" Jen asked Carrie. "There is a state park not far with riding trails along the ocean. It's so beautiful. We can borrow my neighbor's horses. What do you think?"

"Sure, I would love to. When can we go?"

"Tomorrow morning. I'll call Sandra, make sure she's okay with it."

Jen dialed the phone. "Sandra, this is Jen. How are you?"

"I'm good, Jen. How are you doing?"

"Quarantine has been lifted so right now, I'm looking for a little diversion. My friend is here from Australia and I want to take her riding at Montana De Oro. They euthanized my horses. Could I borrow two of yours? I've seen them work at the gatherings and think they would be great rides for Carrie and myself."

"Sure," replied Sandra. "That would be fine. I heard about what happened. I'm sorry, Jen."

"Can we borrow your tack? I'm not ready to go through my own horse equipment yet. Too many memories."

"Yes, and you can use my trailer too."

"Thanks, Sandra. I appreciate this from the bottom of my heart. I am starting to feel, to enjoy things again. I'll be there tomorrow morning, around seven."

"You're welcome, Jen. I'm glad you're getting back on your feet."

Jen hung up the phone. "It's all set," she told Carrie.

The next morning Jen and Carrie drove to Sandra's place.

Jen waved hello to Sandra as she pulled up to the barn.

"Hey Sandra, this is my friend Carrie. She's from Australia."

After attaching the horse trailer to the pickup, the three went to meet the horses, Lenny and Sonny. They were well trained and walked easily into the trailer. Sandra showed Jen and Carrie which tack belonged to which horse and waved them off.

"Have a good time!"

"We will, bye."

Arriving in Montana de Oro State Park, Jen drove past the overnight horse camp to the horse trailer parking lot. The lot was on a bluff about 50 feet above the beach.

"I love the smell of salt water, and the noise of the waves!" Carrie said.

"Me too," Jen said, taking a deep breath she smiled.

The girls brushed their horses, cleaned dirt and pebbles from their hooves, then saddled and bridled them.

"I want to take you to the highest spot in the park first," Jen said as she pulled herself into the saddle. "We will soon know if Sandra's horses are in shape!"

"How so?" asked Carrie.

"See that hill? We're at fifty feet elevation. We'll ride the to the top of the thirteen hundred fifty-foot hill in two miles.

"What is that in meters?"

"I think it's about 450 meters."

"I see your point. I'm glad I'm riding, and not walking."

"Follow me, Carrie," Jen said, as she clicked at Sonny and squeezed her knees, the go forward cue for trained horses.

But Carrie was still not fully seated in her saddle and when Lenny jumped forward to keep up with his friend, Carrie lurched backward.

"Jen, Luv!" she yelled. "Slowdown! I haven't been riding for some time. Take your time with me for the first bit."

"Okay, Carrie. Sorry. I got too excited; it's been a while for me too."

Sandra's horses were in good shape; they took the uphill at a steady walk. This allowed time for Jen and Carrie to appreciate the wildflowers as well as the scenery. Montana De Oro's magnificence increased exponentially the higher the horses went.

The first part of the trail was a slow rise to the hills. This bench land was populated with native lupines, poppies, and Indian paintbrush.

As the trail rose, more and more of the coastline became visible. Soon they could see where the bench lands dropped off onto the beaches. It was beautiful today; the surf turned into mist from waves relentlessly smashing into the dark rocks lying on the beaches.

"Carrie! Stop a minute. Look over there. See that sand spit?"

"Yes."

"We'll be there in a half hour. And do you see that giant round dome shaped rock on the other side of the sand spit? That's Morro Rock."

At the top they stopped and let the horses rest. "Oh, It's so beautiful!" Carrie exclaimed. "Half of what I see is deep blue ocean, the other half is brush covered hills with the brown, sandy beach and white capped waves dividing the two."

"Well, girlfriend, let's go down and see that beach," Jen said as she remounted Sonny. Sonny immediately wanted to go forward, but Jen held him back until Carrie was ready. The horses had more energy in their stride, making it down in half the time.

They took a water break at base camp and headed for the beach.

"Ready, Carrie?"

"Yep," she said, hurrying into her saddle. The horses followed deeply rutted trails with sand dunes on either side of them. Beach grasses had stabilized the dunes somewhat. However, there were still a few areas where shifting, sliding sand covered the ground. Here, the wind had carved a series of solid waves into the exposed surface.

"Keep off the sculpted areas, Carrie. The deep sand is too hard on the horses."

As the beach dunes diminished they came upon a heavier impacted, tide-influenced region where the sand was path. But the path was trickier because of the giant boulders strewn all around.

"Why are these boulders here?" Carrie asked. "Were they placed to break the waves?"

"No, the boulders fell from the cliff behind us. As the waves chew at the bench lands, they recede a little every year," Jen replied, pointing to the cliff supporting the parking lot fifty feet above. The relentless waves pounded the base daily at high tide.

As they carefully walked the horses between and across the boulders the dry sand gave way to glistening sand packed tightly from the water. This was what Jen was looking forward to. Urging Sonny into a canter Lenny quickly realized he was being left behind and galloped to catch up. Both horses sprinted full out down the hard, compact beach for a mile before stopping.

"Carrie let's walk the horses into the water."

"Oh, okay," she replied. "Show me," she said. Pulling on the reins Carrie stopped her horse to watch Jen.

Standing in her saddle Jen made sure she was well balanced in her seat before urging Sonny into the water's edge. The horse didn't like it when his feet disappeared in the advancing waves and began a sideways dance in protest of the command. But Jen persevered; she would not let Sonny turn around. Every time he tried, she reined him back around in a circle clicking at him and squeezing her knees until he was facing the ocean again.

Sonny snorted and fidgeted, but eventually he did as he was asked and took four more steps into the waves snaking around his feet. Jen patted and reassured him. When they were standing knee deep in the water, Jen made him walk parallel to the water's edge. "You need to try this!" She yelled at Carrie, as the taller swells lapped her boots.

Carrie tried the same maneuvers on Lenny. She could get him to walk among the waves curling along the sand, but he wouldn't get his feet submerged.

Jen came onto the beach. "Let's canter down the sand spit to Morro Rock," she suggested. After a brisk, thirty-minute ride they came to the end of the sand spit. The small strait formed between the sand spit and Morro Rock allowed boats from Morro Bay Harbor access to the ocean.

"That finishes our tour for today," Jen said as they stood watching the boats and admiring the beauty of the Bay. As they galloped back to the Montana De Oro trails, Jen said: "Here, let's get up out of the sand." She turned inland on a trail that led right into the horse camp area, where people could camp overnight near the beach with their horses.

"Do you smell that, Jen?"

"Smell what?"

"It smells like Australia! It must be the eucalyptus forest we are going into! It makes me miss home."

Jen stopped and sniffed. "Yeah it makes me want to go there too," she said connecting the fragrance to her overseas trip. "We have several of these eucalypt stands throughout the area. I read the railroads planted a lot of them in the last part of the nineteenth century. Everyone wanted to get rich selling lumber from the fast-growing eucalyptus, but the lumber really wasn't good enough to use for timber, the wood would twist and warp too much."

"You should go back, with me, Jen," Carrie suggested.

Jen stopped. "To Australia?"

"Yes, I think it would be good for you."

"I don't know. I hadn't thought of that."

"Just for a month, or even two weeks, Jen. Think about it."

"I worry about my animals. They are my responsibility, you know?"

"Jen, you have no horses and Honey has your dogs. What else are you worried about?"

"The sugar gliders, Carrie."

"Where are they now?"

"I moved them to Sandra's place before quarantine. She says they're doing fine, but some of them have escaped. I'm worried she doesn't know what she's doing. It'll ruin my breeding project."

"Jen, you can restart the program when you return"

"Yes, but she doesn't know how they got out. I'm afraid she might lose them all, and the thought of them dying because I brought them here horrifies me."

"Gliders live in eucalypt forest, Jen. You just told me there are a lot of them in California."

"Well, yes, there are eucalypt stands all along Hwy 101 into the Monterey area. And I believe they have been planted all the way down to L.A. That makes me feel better, Carrie."

"And I've read the University of Santa Cruz has the largest collection of Australian plants outside of Australia," Carrie added. "Your escaped sugar gliders will be fine on their own."

Chapter 32

Back to Australia

Once the decision was made, Jen prepared, for her trip to Australia. When they were ready, Honey Rose drove Jen and Carrie to San Francisco the day before their flight as they had an early departure and decided to stay overnight in a hotel by the airport. They took Honey to lunch at a restaurant in the hotel. It was a sad lunch for Honey and for Jen.

"I'll be back, Honey," Jen said. "Don't worry. I bought a round trip ticket."

Honey laughed. "You do whatever you need to do to get better, Jen. Everything will be fine at home. We'll just miss you, that's all."

When it was time to go, Jen and Carrie walked Honey to her car. Jen took Honey in her arms and held her for a long time.

"You have been a good friend to me," Honey said. 'I know there was some reason we found each other, and we'll find each other again."

"You mean in our next life?" Jen asked, laughing.

"Well, yes. But let's keep in touch in this one, okay?"
"Don't forget, you still have my dogs, so you know I'll be back. Keep a light on for me. I love you."

There were tears in Honey's eyes." I love you too Jen, very much."

She turned to Carrie. "Goodbye Carrie. I'm so glad you came. Stay safe, and make sure Jen calls me."

Carrie hugged Honey. "We'll call you when we get to Brisbane. You drive safely. Bye Honey."
Honey drove away, and Jen and Carrie walked into the hotel.
The flight to Australia was a long one. Jen had forgotten just how long it was, but it was more fun with company. She and Carrie talked, and slept, and ate their way across the sky. They were really ready to stretch their legs by the time they landed. It was a

full flight, and two other jumbo jets had unloaded about the same time their flight did. The lines in customs were long and slow. The customs' area exited into a long hall that led directly outside. As they turned down the hall, Jen was having trouble with the wheels on her luggage. She had stopped to fix them when she heard Carrie call "Billy!"

Jen looked up and saw Billy standing in the doorway, silhouetted by the bright daylight outside. Her heart skipped as she thought "Here is my new beginning." She was already glad she had come back.

Chapter 33

Another Colic

On his way to town to do errands, Chuck noticed Dr. Evans' truck was in his neighbor's paddock. "Hey Earl," he paused as he drove by. "Why is Doc here?"

"My mare is down with colic and she keeps trying to lay down."

"Oh, well Doc's a good one; he'll take care of it."

As Chuck drove away, Rory waved. When he walked to the mare and put his thermometer in her anus, he found she had a fever. He looked at her nostrils. Frothy blood was dripping from both nostrils. "I don't goddamn believe this," he mumbled, as he backed away from the horse. "Earl! Drop the lead rope right now!"

"But she might roll because of her colic."

"Earl! You need to listen closely. This horse may have Hendra; it's a disease that will kill you! Do you remember what happened to Randy Bianchi? Just drop the lead and walk to me, right now."

Earl did as he was told. "You really think this is the same thing, Doc?"

"I don't know for sure, but we can't take any chances. Now, get out of the pen and make sure all the gates are closed. I have to get some supplies and help in town, but, do not go into that pen while I'm gone, Earl. Okay?"

"Sure, okay, Doc."

Rory was shaking.

God dammit, I don't believe this… this can't be Hendra! Where the hell is this coming from?

As Rory got into his truck, Earl asked: "How long will you be, Doc?"

"Long enough to get the right people and supplies together."

When Chuck got into cell phone range, he called Honey Rose. "Honey, can you do me a favor?"

"Sure, Chuck. What's up?"

"I need you to drive to my place to make sure Bulldog was put in the house. I don't like to leave him outside when I'm not there."

"Sure, no problem."

"Hey, Honey, I saw the Doc at Earls' place."

"Yeah, he's doing ranch calls today so I'm taking the calls from home."

When Honey drove to Chuck's house, Bulldog was hanging around the back door. She let him in the house and paused on the way back to her car. She could hear a continuous high-pitched yip-yip-yip coming from the eucalyptus trees. *Those are Jen's sugar gliders!"* she said to herself. *Jen will be happy to know they're still alive.*

About the Author

Dr. Jim Aarons has a unique view of the world, having spent a lifetime, doctoring animals. Since graduating in 1982, from California's UC Davis School of Veterinary Medicine, he has been responsible for the physical and mental soundness of a vast variety of critters, and as their human friends.

With his unique and up-front writing style, Dr. Jim artfully mixes the softness of romance against the harsh canvas of science and history. Pulling ideas from a long life of work with animals, he is sharing his experiences from zoos and ostrich hatcheries, horse stud farms, cattle round-ups, cow dairies, and companion animal medicine cases. With an intriguing, unending palette of horses, medicine, and human nature he has created the Katie Reynolds series, a saga of our early attempts to find a real reason for us to be here.

Dr. Jim has worked diligently to craft fictional stories that are not just your garden variety of veterinary tales. His books include his first attempt, "Fear of Failure" an autobiography, followed by the Katie Reynolds series.

Thank you for giving me a whirl and have a great read!

******** "Life is better with horses." *********

The Katie Reynolds Series

I have penned a saga of stories celebrating history, culture, religion, and life in different countries and in different times, yet all related.

The first book, **K'aalógii, The Butterfly Boy** introduces Rory and Katie, who are the main characters throughout all of the books. They are in veterinary school, where they meet, fall in love, and go through ordeals made harder because of their cultural differences. He is a white dude from southern California, smart, but clueless. Katie is a Navajo Indian; they call themselves the Diné. The story has horses, cultural conflicts, and histories wrapped around Katie and Rory's love.

Yé'iitsoh Omen, the second book takes them back to Katie's native Dinétah where evil spirits, both Ute and Navajo are on a tirade to push her out. Temporarily defeated she joins Rory at his veterinary practice in California where he shows her the beauty of the paradise he has stumbled onto. He reopens an old veterinary clinic to entice her to settle in with him.

Yet Katie cannot shake the call to return to learning, sure she can help her people if only she knew more. But she is falling deeply in love with Rory and needs to find a balance between her desires and his future wishes.

Rory proposes to her hoping the promise of marriage will plug the gap she feels.

In **Death from Down Under** Rory has to deal with Jen, an old girlfriend, and now a client, who needs to ship dogs to Australia. Well, Jen, is acting like Jen, which means bad shit. She ends up smuggling sugar gliders in from Australia, causing an outbreak of Hendra virus among horses and vets and horse owners here in California. This smuggling creates a problem in Jen's marriage when the virus kills her husband Randy.

In **Tsegi Ruins** the spirits are pushing harder. They want something from Katie, yet she's unsure what it is. They don't want to kill her otherwise she'd be toast by now. The answer becomes clearer following an all-night peyote tipi rite. Rory realizes the tug on Katie might pull her from him, and he ups the ante by marrying his sweetheart.

Nonetheless her quest to understand the ravages of disease continues to push her to further her education.

The saga diverges in the next two books, **The First Altar,**

158

and **The Inconvenient Goddess**, when the story moves into Europe and the Middle East.

René and Katie are called to Iraq to stem an outbreak of Brucellosis. Rory and Katie marry, and Marol offers them passage in her jet as a honeymoon gift, allowing Rory to find a place nearer Katie by helping Marol set up her ostrich egg import company in Israel.

There are always wars happening in the Middle East. Now Katie and René find themselves overwhelmed in the mountains above Mosul. They hide inside an ancient temple to escape the gunfire. A grenade blows them back in time, to 1330 BC, when the Egyptians ruled the area. Katie, having suddenly appeared, becomes Inanna, an ancient Goddess. She learns to use the power handed to her and eventually becomes Ištar, Astarte, and eventually Aphrodite, but those things happen in the three books after this one.

Rory continues to breathe and function after Katie disappears, and finds himself in his own book, called **Cocaine Eggs**. In this book, cocaine is smuggled into the U.S. inside ostrich eggs heading into a USDA-sanctioned quarantine station. This story is loaded with sex, drugs, and cool chapters like shark hunting, the Florida Keys, Las Vegas, New Orleans. I introduce Silk Road and Bitcoin here, and how the guy who ran the thing was busted. Did I say sex? A Playboy model has Rory come out to certify her tiger enclosure, really.

In **Gods and Mortals**, Katie gains more power in 1330 BC, learning the ropes, and showing the ancients how to do cool stuff, like c-sections on people. Mercifully she finds that they have an anesthesia made with an opium-based elixir. It becomes kick-ass when mixed with Old Štyle Šumerian Beer. This is the book where she falls in love with Thoma, a charioteer in the Mitanni maryannu, the elite horsemen and warriors of that time.

Queen of the Orontes picks up right when Katie wakes up from being knocked unconscious at the end of that last book. She marries Thoma, René marries Citri, while war noises between the

Egyptians and the Hittites are increasing. There is a climactic chariot battle at Kadesh, where Ramses II falsely declares victory over Katie's team. Her team has an advantage because she is a real veterinarian, and finds a fellow named Kikkuli, an ancient horse whisperer who makes kick-ass chariots. I didn't pick Kikkuli's name because it was close to kick-ass, he was a real guy who wrote state-of-the-art horse husbandry tablets and shipped them to King Šuppiluliuma, the Hittite ruler. Look it up.

Back to Katie, in her next story **Ivory Kingdom**. When Tutankhamun, the King Tut we all know and love, died in 1327 BCE, his young widowed wife Ankhesenamun wrote to Šuppiluliuma I. She asked for help finding a new husband and King. (This also is actual history.) Katie is summoned, and she packs up Thoma, her husband to deliver the prodigal son Zananza to the Egyptian widow. The ship breaks apart in a storm off the western coast of Cypress, where the survivors land at Paphos, the birthplace of the Greek Goddess Aphrodite. Katie goes there to find her husband. She has already filled the shoes of Inanna, Ištar, and Astarte, and now becomes Aphrodite.

Welcome to my world. I invite you to be part of it. The stories continue in my head and will become real as I write them.

www.ingramcontent.com/pod-product-compliance
Lightning Source LLC
Chambersburg PA
CBHW071524170626
46811CB00007B/2940